I0553367

SIDE ROADS

SIDE ROADS

A DARK FICTION COLLECTION

RACHEL A. BRUNE

DEVIL
TREE
press

Side Roads
Copyright © 2021 by Rachel A. Brune

All rights reserved.

No part of this book may be reproduced in any form or by any electronic or mechanical means, including information storage and retrieval systems, without written permission from the author, except for the use of brief quotations in a book review.

"Shadow Pool" was originally published in *Imaginarium*, October 2013, Issue 2.

"IronFae" was originally published in *Aoife's Kiss*, March 2013, Issue 44.

"The Carnival Ghost" was originally published in *Hideous Progeny: Classic Horror Goes Punk*, Writerpunk Press, 2018.

"The Terrible, Vast Pyre of Chief Machinist Kirlisoveyitch" was originally published in *Dark Moon Digest*, October 2012, Issue 9.

"Readers" was originally published in *T. Gene Davis's Speculative Fiction Blog*, February 2014.

"Finding Things After You're Gone" was originally published in *Stardust: Always*, June 2016.

"Terminal Leave" was originally published in *O-Dark-Thirty*, Winter 2016, Volume 4, Number 2.

"The Peacemaker" was originally published in *Fantasy Scroll Magazine*, September 2014, Issue 3.

Published by Devil Tree Press
Print ISBN: 978-1-952388-05-7
Ebook ISBN: 978-1-952388-06-4
Cover design by James at GoOnWrite.com

This one is for my Bugs...

CONTENTS

CURIOUSER AND CURIOUSER

SUCH A STRANGE HABIT HE HAD, THIS PICKING. PICK, PICK, PICK at skin, at imperfections, at acne, at the scabs that grew over the bone—pick, pick, pick.

He *scratch-itch-scratched* over half-formed scars until they parted, revealing the moist redness underneath, until they healed over thick white tissue.

So strange. So curious. So fragile.

When there came no injury to open the elastic skin, he *itch-scratch-itched* until the door opened under his nails, and he held the hole to his arm to *lick-lick-lick* it closed. Then the scab would form, and he would have his next tic, his next pick, his next trick.

So strange. So curious. So fragile.

For days, he would hold his hands hostage, clip the nails to the quick, flick the little toys that kept his fingers ever moving, ever lickety-spit-quick tap-tapping, and finally, slipping his digits into the mitts that should have kept him from picking. And yet, after a few days, he must needs remove his gloves, his nails grow long again, and he's back at it—pick, pick, pickety-pick.

So strange. So curious. So fragile these creatures who squirmed and cried and twisted and begged with their strange, soft tongues and their curious, delicate bodies.

Whatever would happen if he *pick-pick-picked* to stick— Stick! Stick!—those long, sharp nails just a little ... further under the skin?

SIDE ROADS

I LOCK THE DOOR BEHIND ME. WE'RE IN THE MIDDLE OF nowhere, and there's nothing in the car worth taking, but it's a force of habit. My sunglasses immediately fog up. The air conditioning in the beat-up old Ford works just fine, but the Southern late-summer humidity has me immediately breaking out in a sweat.

The dirt road stretches out before me. The lush green from the water-laden trees presents a thick wall, arching up and over us, cutting out most of the blue. It reminds me of pictures I've seen of South American rain forests, but I wouldn't know. Never seen them in real life. I slap my neck.

"Mosquitoes are thick." The phrase isn't much more than a grunt.

"Yup." I wonder at my traveling partner's sudden chattiness. He doesn't go in much for small talk. It's mostly been sports talk radio when he drives and classic rock when I'm behind the wheel for most of this trip. "Shall we?"

He nods, squinting against the sweat beading on his forehead, dripping down the side of his face. Without warning, he moves forward. The impenetrable green seems to open before him as he slips into the undergrowth.

Grumbling, I follow. Immediately, branches reach out and snag my clothing. A thorny strand wraps itself around my leg, leaving a welt through my cargo pants. I heft the shotgun, the machete slapping against my thigh, and keep an eye on the path as the brush closes behind us. The insect whine grows louder. I'm soaked with sweat, smelling rich loam, rotting things, and the intense aroma of green under the sun.

Then, I smell something different. Something dead, that brings the taste of copper to my mouth. I swallow against the sudden dryness.

My partner doesn't say anything—just catches my eye and points at a spot about twenty yards in front of him. He holds up three fingers, then three more.

Six. It's almost not even worth stopping. If I'd been driving, we'd have kept going. This trip's been just a shade on the too-long side, we're both covered with flop sweat and diner grease, and I need a break. My partner, though, there's no expression on his face as he rips into them, shreds of black and flesh falling to the sides.

It was a creche; I look around trying to find the adults, but they're nowhere to be found, and from the stale-green smell, they've been a long time gone. I move forward to try to help my partner, but with the flash of steel and claws, he's not paying any attention and I stay off to the side and out of the way.

I wouldn't have stopped.

The man lounging behind the counter looks like he might be a little too interested in what I'm buying, but then Jacob comes in from fueling up, and Mr. Local Yokel settles back in his seat. Squinting, he frowns down at the paper spread in front of him, ignoring us. I grab a bottle of Coke from the fridge and pick up a couple bags of pork rinds.

"Anything else?" Yokel doesn't bother looking up.

"Nope."

"Eight twenty-five." He turns the page. "Plus tax."

I hand him a ten spot and dump the few coins he gives back into one of the half dozen charity contribution jars lining the peeling counter surface.

Outside, the sun is heading closer to the horizon, but the heat hasn't waned. If anything, it's gotten warmer. The first gulp of soda runs down my throat cold and delicious. Then the bottle gets warmer and sticky-sweet.

"Ready?" Jacob is a man of few words.

"Let's go." The beat-up Ford doesn't look like much from the outside, but she starts up just fine. It's my turn to drive. I hand Jacob the map. "Let me know when we get closer."

I once had a GPS. Turns out, geo-positioning satellites and Moray Magic don't mix, and now we rely on paper and prior planning.

The sun is just low enough to peek out from below the visor. I squint against the glare as I pull out of the parking lot and accelerate down the deserted road. "What was all that back there?"

Jacob leans back and closes his eyes.

"Seriously, man." The road leads to the highway, and I take the exit a little too fast.

Jacob opens his eyes again to give me a look, the one that says I better not mess up his ride.

"Calm down, killer." I turn to give him a big smile, keeping the road in my peripheral vision. I keep smiling for a few more long seconds ... and then a few more. Finally, he shrugs.

"Few less Blackhearts." He lowers his own visor against the glare. "What's the problem?"

"The problem?" I can't keep the sarcasm out of my voice. Jacob hates sarcasm. "Not only a few less Blackhearts, but we left them in a few more pieces than usual."

"Nest ain't that big, still gotta make sure you get 'em all."

"I'm not arguing that point." What we found in that hollow —let's just say I'll be seeing it when I close my eyes for a long time, turning the image around and around like a picture postcard. One Blackheart on its own is nasty business, and there had been about six or seven living there. "But you killed them and kept going."

"It's a bloody business." There's a note in his voice that sets my nerves on edge—at once cold and empty, and at the same time vicious and eager.

I'm both anticipating and dreading our return; the Director is going to want a full report, and I can't figure if she's going to want to hear all the details of the unplanned stops we've made, or if I'm going to once again be covering for my partner, ignoring his evasions and silently nodding through his half-explanations. This could be the last trip we make together, and I haven't grown tired of this one. Yet.

The sun flares briefly, and I turn, just as the last rays illuminate Jacob's eyes. Beneath the steely gray, the light catches other, deeper cones. Just for a moment, the red glows through, punctuating the slight smile that doesn't conceal the sharp tips of his teeth.

"Are you willing to spill what you need?"

We're heading up to New Jersey. The western route takes us through the mountains. The air here is marginally cooler than it was down east. Today, there's even a hint of rain. The truck grinds and whines with a peculiar rattle every time we hit a particularly steep hill.

Around three in the afternoon, we hit Gettysburg. I never visited here in real life, and I'm looking forward to making a pit stop. Take a piss, pump some gas, stretch our legs.

Jacob ghosts the minute the engine clanks to a halt. One moment he's sitting next to me in the passenger seat, the next he's halfway down the street, leaving me to fill the parking meter and figure out lunch. The heat's not so bad up here. It's still August, but it's overcast and kind of misting out. The humidity seems to have given us a break. I pocket my sunglasses. The rain keeps beading up, and I don't need them anyway.

In this day and age of sci-fi tech and instant communication, the Director likes to use the U.S. Postal Service. Don't ask me why. She's old school like that. Also, hacking is a hobby, but messing with the mail is a federal crime. When we're traveling, we get instructions forwarded to the places we'll be stopping, complete with hand-lettered envelopes and Forever stamps with red-white-and-blue flags. Go America.

I head down to the local P.O. to pick up any mail that's waiting for us, thinking about what kind of food I want for lunch. I always pick up something for Jacob, and then end up eating it myself. I've never seen the guy actually consume anything approved by the FDA, but everyone has weird habits about something. I hate for guys to know I poop. It's a thing.

Anyway, it's right around lunch so of course the Post Office is packed with people trying to run errands on their break from whatever suit-and-tie slavery they're living—or parents and their bored, impatient kids, whining. And who could blame them? I don't want to be there, either.

Still, all that ... humanity ... crawls under my skin. It's hard to focus. Hard to stay calm. Even with the Director's Moray Magic wrapping itself around my nerves.

Finally, it's my turn. The man behind the counter speaks with a Deep South drawl, which is weird, because this is southern Pennsylvania. Not as jarring as it could have been, though. We *have* just spent the last four months recreating Sherman's march, only instead of burning Johnny Reb, we've been exterminating Johnny Blackheart.

"You've got these here pieces of U.S. postal mail," he says, giving "here" and "mail" a few extra syllables. "And that's about it. You have a blessed day."

"Thank you, you too," I answer, voice sweet as honey. Bless his heart.

I decide to wait in the lobby, leaning against one of the counters, tapping the two—*two this time*—envelopes against the palm of my hand. One of them has been addressed to me, as usual. The other is for Jacob. Unusual.

"Are you mad?"

I can't tell if the kid addressing me is a boy or girl. Long-ish blond hair, pre-pubescent, probably around five? Six? Whatever. I'm shit at guessing kids' ages.

"No, honey, I'm not mad," I reassure the small human standing in front of me and look around for whatever parent hasn't yet realized their barnacle has become unattached. "I'm just worried that you're talking to a stranger."

"Maddie, what have I told you about going up to people you don't know?" The man is tall, also blond, and beautiful, with a left hand unadorned by a wedding ring. I'm suddenly alert. Even if my nerves have been blunted, there are some parts of my nature the Director hasn't yet been able to excise.

"It's quite all right." I start my smile, standing up straight, pushing a stray hair behind my ears, hoping I've gotten all the stains out from under my fingernails. "She's not bothering me at all." Next question is for the girl. "And how old are you, Maddie?"

Here comes the bout of shyness, when the child realizes that their gambit for attention has actually succeeded.

"Go ahead, Maddie," her father urges, "you can tell her."

Clearly, my gambit for attention is also succeeding.

"I'm five," she squeaks out, hiding behind his leg.

"She is so cute," I tell her dad. I'm starting to fall in love.

"Ready?" Jacob's harsh barking breaks me out of my reverie. My heart drops. So many lost opportunities.

"Well, you and your dad have a wonderful day!" I give her dad a smile that I hope conveys how sorry I am to leave. Matching blonds are my favorite.

We're back in the old Ford and on our way to New Jersey, stuck in traffic outside of Harrisburg, before I remember the letter. I'm dreaming about my blonds, regretting the compulsion that keeps me from using my blade in my own interests. That's when it hits me. There had been something for Jacob from the Director.

It's on the tip of my tongue to tell him. He'll be pissed that I forgot. But I could say later that I just remembered, so I'm not that worried. I'm more worried about what she sent him. He's never gotten a letter.

I sink back into the seat, tapping the wheel impatiently, waiting for the traffic to resolve itself. Why do cities insist on doing road work that shuts down lanes during rush hour? And why is there always a cop car with its lights flashing and nobody sitting in it? Wouldn't it be cheaper to just get a disco ball or something?

We didn't get to keep anything from our time before the

Director, when she re-connected our synapses and used Moray Magic to electro-shock our nerves back to life. But my memories were never contingent on physical objects. Rather, I took memory snapshots, and saved them for moments such as these.

Jacob sits up, sniffing. I groan inwardly, reluctantly, catching his eye. Seriously? Here? He nods, that curious red flash burning and then fading.

"Okay, fine." I take the next exit, merging east on a highway just as wide and fast-running as the northern route we've been on.

He directs me by grunts and jerks of his hand. It's effective, probably because it's what I'm used to. Still annoying, though.

From the interstate, we turn off onto another highway, and then onto another road that's still two lanes in each direction. I don't know why we never find these things in more populated areas. Would be nice to take out a nest in, say, a spa resort. Or someplace with a Jacuzzi. Ew. Jacob in a Jacuzzi. Shudder. Never mind.

The two-lane meanders for a while, heading generally north and east, so at least we're not going completely out of our way. In fact, we're making better time than we would have by staying on the interstate.

After about forty-five minutes or so, we take a side road, which then forks into two more little side roads, neither of them paved. Jacob grunts at the left fork, so I turn that way. The road devolves into a dirt path that eventually dead ends in the front lawn of some long-deserted structure.

It looks like an abandoned two-story home. Or, coulda been a warehouse. Or a meth lab. Hell, this is rural Pennsylvania, so it's possible it could have been all three at once.

I get the chainsaw out of the trunk, sling it across my back (my own design—I'm pretty proud of it, wish I'd thought of it before) and strap my trusty machete to my hip. Check the blade. Sharp as ever.

Jacob just grins and does the thing where his teeth elongate until his mouth bursts full of sharp, pointed fangs. His fingernails lengthen, becoming harder and ending in razor sharp claws. Whatever the Director stuffed into his meat husk, it definitely wasn't human.

"After you," I tell him.

He chuckles. The only time he ever does that is right before we go to work. I don't know if he thinks something's funny or just really loves his job.

There's still a little daylight, but the sun is almost completely under the horizon, and the light doesn't make it inside. The building is dark and smells like animals have been living—and dying—in it. The door slams behind us. I can't use Moray Magic, but there are perks to being its creature. I close my eyes, focus, and when I open them, I can see in the dark.

It's not totally effective. I mean, it's not like it's brilliant daytime in there. Everything looks kind of grainy and fuzzy, glowing around the edges like a cheap nightvision option on a video camera. But it's enough.

Jacob turns, the red glow behind his eyes much more noticeable. He points to the left, where a staircase leads to the upper level. Apparently, I'm to go to the right, poke around the ground floor. Sure thing, even though I'm supposed to be in charge. He always picks the area with more of them, and I'm not going to argue. I call it delegating.

After a cursory search, I wonder if Jacob actually picked the area with all of them. I haven't seen a single sign that hints at Blackhearts hibernating here. This close, they usually drop some spoor—blood, rotting body parts, anything you might see in a cheap horror film. But this place is clean. Not clean like the maid just came, but like horrific shadow monsters aren't living there.

I'm about to give up and go sit in the Ford and wait for Jacob. A loud ruckus breaks out over my head. Straining to see up the stairs, I'm rewarded by a hiss somewhere in the air above me and to the right. The hiss is followed by a meaty thunk in the face by something cold and wet.

"Damn it, Jacob!" Using the bottom of my shirt, I swipe at my face, trying to clean it. "Next time give me some warning."

Asshole. The only response is a chuckle and more whisper-thunks. Something's going on upstairs. Jacob is a silent hunter; the claws and teeth don't make much noise, and his victims rarely get a chance to even scream in reaction.

I blink the rest of the gore from my eyes. There is a soft glow that partially illuminates the room I'm standing in. A door hangs off its hinges across the hall. I can make out a low, sloping ceiling. Looks like stairs? Maybe a basement? Worth checking out.

The smell of dead things hits my nose as soon as I step down the first stair. Soft rustlings and mutterings suddenly become still, as if whatever's down there notices my presence.

It's not one of the biggest nests I've taken care of, but there's more than one, and they're big, too. The first Blackheart unfolds itself out of what appeared at first glance to be a large pile of moldy blankets.

It lifts itself onto all fours, all tattered cloth and corporeal shadows. We've seen them in all stages of development, but this is the furthest along I've faced. Almost all of its limbs are intact. A large protuberance on one end waves back and forth. The effect is that of a big, black dog, sniffing blindly at a barely perceived threat.

I let myself go silent in the shadows, waiting—for the Blackheart to reveal my target, for any others to stir and join him. Movements begin under the pile, slowly at first, then gathering momentum and form.

The first pokes itself up. This is a new-ish one, only a baby. Warmth floods me. Perhaps I've found a family—mother and child? No, surely, father and child. Yes. Now I'm primed and ready to go.

Two more Hearts stir. The father Heart nuzzles them, and they subside. Guess he's not convinced the danger has passed.

I grip the machete and slide it soundlessly from the leather scabbard. Just a few more feet, just a little more...

The Blackheart rears up on his hind legs. He's big. Head almost touches the ceiling. There, in the center of his chest, beats my target.

The meat is long dead, a heart stolen from a corpse. Blood flows, black and liquified. Under my Moray sight, it pumps vividly through the veins that still cling to the purloined flesh.

The machete's blade doesn't flicker or flash. The steel simply pierces the heart. I withdraw it, tugging as it resists the blade, then puncture the heart again. The Blackheart freezes, writhes. The thumping, flailing limbs force the blood to spray faster. I dodge a blind punch, a wildly-thrown kick.

With the blood slicking the handle, I lose my grip, and the Blackheart rears up, backing away. No matter. None of the others are of any size to worry me.

Bringing the chainsaw around to my front, I drop one side of the sling and pull the chain. My trusty partner roars to life. The vibrations under my palms have me wet and sweaty. It's at these moments I understand Jacob and his wild glee.

With the powertool buzz putting a spring in my step, I wade into the fray. The trick is to ignore the limbs and concentrate on slicing into the heart. That's where these creatures begin, and that's where they must end.

Piercing's not enough, though. The father Blackheart

retreats as I approach. There's nowhere for him to go. He paws at the machete, still extruding from his chest. The roar of the chainsaw gives him something to focus on. But he can't get around the harsh blade.

Ignoring him for the moment, I creep to the child. Crooning a soft, reassuring tone, I slash with the tool. The loyal chainsaw performs as expected and cuts the target Heart in two. A few more slices, and its heart lies in the requisite quarters. I kick at it to scatter the pieces—not technically necessary, but I'm always superstitious that they'll reform behind me like some resurrecting horror movie monster.

Striding to the mound where I previously spotted move-ment, I stand over it with the chainsaw and kick until I've uncovered two more targets. These are barely much more than corpse hearts with their small shadows attached, hiding under actual tattered blankets.

With the children dispatched, it's time to finish the father. The Blackheart sits, slumped against the back wall. He offers no resistance as I pull the machete from his chest and slice and dice. I kick those pieces apart as well.

Briefly, my heart pangs for my former life.

I shut down the chainsaw and use one of the blankets to roughly wipe the blade of the machete before re-sheathing it. I'll clean it more thoroughly later. Chainsaw re-slung, I take a moment to just stand and observe. More than once, I've caught a Blackheart trying to slink away after it thought I'd left.

Huh.

The basement is well and truly painted with black gore. I let out a shuddering breath. Jacob waits above me somewhere in the dark. He can keep waiting. I close my eyes, embedding this picture in my memory, and slide it into the spot next to Jacob's hollow from before.

The indulgences of my past are forbidden to me, but the Director knew whose spirit she stuffed into this meat husk. I am good at my job.

By the time we get back on the road, we're so far north that the map tells us we should just keep going, hook up with Route 80 to get over the Delaware River, instead of our normal route.

"We'll get in around five in the morning." There's no oncoming traffic, so I flip on the high beams. Jacob doesn't respond, but I didn't think he would. "The Director hates side projects."

I don't expect a response, but I get one.

"Did you read your letter?"

The syntax throws me. "*My* letter?"

He tosses two pieces of paper on the bench seat between us. I don't look—it's dark in the cab. "Help me out, Master of Silence." Hopefully, he doesn't notice the shake in my voice. "What's it say?"

The red glow behind his eyes intensifies, reflecting in the windshield. Reminds me of a sniper's laser target. I'm not going to like it. I feel that shark-tipped grin sitting next to me in the darkness.

A young deer appears on the side of the road, its dappled coat betraying its juvenile status. Late birth. Should have lost those spots this late in the year. I slow. Deer never show up by themselves. Sure enough, the high beams catch the tapetum glow of the rest of the herd, safely tucked into the woods bordering the winding road.

After a mile of silence, it's obvious I'm going to have to read the damn letter myself. Whatever. The road is deserted. I slow and flip on the overhead light.

Switching my attention back and forth from the road to the paper, I make out the curt message.

Huh. After I finish the page, I flip it over. There's nothing on the other side. I check the road again, then look back down. Jacob's handed me his letter as well. I give it a quick once-over, then reach up and turn out the light.

"Well, that's a hell of a thing."

I put my foot back down on the gas, gunning the engine. The turn for the interstate is coming up, and I don't feel like talking anymore.

I've never taken Jacob for a man of honor. He's a creature of violence, sudden and lethal. He can be counted on to kill what needs to be killed. To be truthful, it doesn't come from a sense of duty. Instead, he emanates a vicious glee, a sort of macabre can-do spirit. It makes him an efficient, effective partner. But honorable? No. And definitely not one to give an opponent a fighting chance.

Yet, there on the seat between us—my letter and his. The Director has charged us each with the same task. Mine says:

NLT 0700 31 AUG: Arrival at LOCATION ZULU.
INTERIM LOCATION: None.
Target arrival: Within normal parameters.
ADD'L Indicators: Arrive only Paradox Bravo.

Paradox Bravo. That's me. My name has faded. Jacob is Paradox Delta. I called him Jacob after my favorite family from the time before. Jacob Father had been full of life, vibrant, his ... my mind is drifting. There had been another Jacob, Paradox Charlie. I had received a similar message and scattered his remains over the wreckage of the last Blackheart nest we'd eliminated together. He'd turned his back to my chainsaw, and I had re-lived the fantasy of my old life.

Now, this double message. The Director's playing some kind of game, and I'll be damned if I can figure out what.

Jacob's message reads: Arrive only Paradox Delta. Is she pitting us against each other? Are we to claw and slice until one meat husk remains? Is it a test? Have we somehow failed in any task she's set us? Have I failed in the exercise of some duty I didn't realize was mine?

The bridge across the river looms ahead of us. Once we enter the state, we'll have about an hour and a half to decide how to approach, what to do. I'm not good at this.

I spent my life and death blissfully unaware of the existence of any sort of magic, let alone the Moray practitioners. Instead, I'd spent my time with my families, ten in total, until the last Jacob. He'd been my incomplete Jacob, the father who turned out to be the warrior, and sent me on my final journey.

Sure, there'd been talk of my mental competence, and mitigating factors, but my public defender—a woman named Maria who didn't understand that I loved Jacob, and didn't want to deny what we'd had—had been able to prove only that there was no reason for anyone not to believe that I had transformed all my precious families. The twelve men and women returned my fate. I refused all appeals. I had waited my whole life to be transformed, and finally I was sent to join my Jacobs.

The needle sliding into my arm was an orgasm.

I'd always pretty much doubted any kind of God talk anyone had ever tried to shove down my throat. Turns out I was right. There's not much after dead. Just ... nothing. Sorry for any church folk just tuning in.

Until the Director ripped me from the nothing and stuffed all of me back into a meat husk.

I am her Paradox Bravo, the paradox who lived. Alpha was weak, and he didn't live. Paradox Charlie was unpleasant, and clung to too many of his old habits. I'd been too eager to give him the name Jacob, and regretted it. I was glad to rip him apart. But Paradox Delta, my new Jacob, *he* was perfect.

I forget what the Director named him. He wasn't human. His spirit was formed of something else. A windy-windo-something; she hadn't told me, but I'd listened at the door as she spoke into her journal.

Wendigo. That was it. I'd looked it up online once, stopping at a local library to use their computers for a few minutes. I'd managed to find some information before the Moray Magic had fried the machine's internal circuits and shut down the row of networked computers, sparking and hissing.

We are a good pair, and we kill Blackhearts like it's our job, and Jacob found this cool truck and got it running so we could ride in style, and I don't know why the Director would send us this message. And I don't know why, if Jacob read it first, I'm still alive.

We haven't been this far north in six months. I've forgotten that autumn comes early in the mountains, even if only at night. The fog creeps down the valley, hinting at the deep dark soil and the first tinge of gold that comes to limn the leaves. It will all be burned off by morning, back to the warmth and heat of a slow-lingering summer, but it's enough to remind us that the dead time of the year will arrive before we know it. Before we're ready.

Location Zulu is a fancy term for a split-level ranch house at the end of a long side road that winds through some old farm fields and cuts off past a recently abandoned lake community. There used to be a summer camp at the entrance years ago, but the land had been foreclosed and then abandoned, and it finally deteriorated past the point of no return. A malaise hangs over the area; the buildings, now gang-tagged and littered with the remnants and debris of teenagers having sex and getting high, are sinking into the fields of weeds and new-growth trees that grow up and around them more every year. The entrance to the road is almost hidden beneath it all, which suits the Director just fine.

My foot lifts off the gas pedal almost involuntarily. The Ford slows, and I search for the secluded spot where we typically park. There's not much I know about Moray Magic, other than the fact that the Director uses it and it causes any networked electronics to commit suicide. The Ford is old enough that it escapes punishment, but in any case, we're not allowed to drive up. We always park in the creepy old summer camp and walk the rest of the way in.

In the past hour, I've thought of a thousand questions, and discarded all of them. I keep expecting Jacob to lunge at me in the dark, claws extended, teeth reaching for my neck. I don't know, maybe he's been waiting until now.

Come to think of it, if I'm going to make my move, now's the time.

The same thought might be occurring to him.

Shit.

I pull the Ford into an old shed, completely hidden in the undergrowth that has camouflaged it. If you didn't know it was there, you'd never have guessed that a mostly intact structure was hidden in the grove of poison sumac and black walnut trees.

With a turn of the key, I kill the engine. It sputters to silence. Now is the time I expect to have some kind of—not a heart-to-heart, this *is* Jacob—but some sort of ... conversation? Planning session? Agreement? Something.

Nothing. Jacob hops out of the cab like nothing unordinary has happened. I leave the keys in the truck and follow after. Are we getting weapons? I feel like we should be getting weapons. Except Jacob doesn't have weapons.

My eyes adjust quickly, in time to see Jacob has assumed full-on wendigo mode. Claws extended, sharp teeth extruding from his too-full mouth, eyes glowing deeper and brighter red than I've ever seen before. He's even grown a couple of inches taller, I'm pretty sure.

Shit.

"Get your shit."

The teeth get in the way, and the words come out with much spitting and drooling. Okay. We're doing weapons. I strap the machete to my hip and sling the chainsaw. A tiny bit of gore clings to the teeth from our unexpected side road, but it should be fine. Moray Magic doesn't give a crap about chainsaws.

Once again, I'm supposed to be taking the lead, but Jacob strides off in the direction of Location Zulu. I hurry to catch up, and the two of us march toward the Director and, with luck, answers. And maybe not killing each other.

———

I'm not sure what's going to happen when we try to attack the Director. I'm pretty sure that's Jacob's plan. Will we collapse like stringless marionettes once the one who brought us to life with her Magic is gone? Is it even possible to kill the woman?

She's not even my type. But I think I can do it. Maybe Jacob will do it, and then we'll just go on from there, driving until we find a side road with another nest of Blackhearts and do that until our meat husks fall apart. Sure. That would be a good life. I could see us doing that until we achieved some kind of redemption for our former lives.

Or just until we got bored.

Maybe I could head back to Gettysburg and wait at the Post Office to see if my blond Jacob comes back.

A faint glow appears behind the trees not too far down the road. The once-paved road has decayed into cracked asphalt as nature continues its reclamation process. I'm not sure if it's the morning sun or something else—what time does the sun come up around here? I have no idea. The trees crowd in all around us, arching over our heads, obscuring the sky. Any hint of autumn fades as a wet, humid warmth grows around us.

My hand grips the machete harder, sweat slicking the handle.

The trees part. Before us, an incongruous site. The glow comes from the strings and strings of white Christmas lights strung all around the house and the two oak trees that stand in the yard.

The Director sits in a broken old lawn chair on the small, square concrete porch outside the front door. At first, I think that the front of the house has somehow become some sort of lake, as it's dark, and writhing. What the hell?

Jacob hisses and the waves stop, freeze, then continue their undulating movements.

Shit. Holy shit. The woman is literally sitting in a giant pool of Blackhearts. I'm confused. Do we start shredding

Hearts? Are we supposed to save her? What the hell is going on?

I unsling the chainsaw and start 'er up. It seems like the best possible answer to a wide range of scenarios.

The Director says nothing. Jacob is similarly laconic. I shrug. There is one thing I know how to do.

Chainsaw at the ready, I wade forward into the mass of Blackhearts. Their limbs clutch at me, tearing like thorny branches at my legs and thighs.

Except for the roar and stutter of the chainsaw, the morning is quiet and peaceful. A few birds have begun to greet the day. It's otherwise silent as I grunt and cuss.

Sweat sticks my shirt to my back and runs down between my breasts. The Blackhearts are eddying and swirling, even more agitated. The majority of them aren't trying to attack. Instead, they seem to be crawling and creeping away as fast as they can, only to be stopped at the edge of the umbra cast by the twinkly Christmas lights.

The chainsaw has started to get blunted. I haven't had a chance to sharpen it in a while, and it catches and sticks against the meat and muscle at the center of the creatures.

I'm not making any progress. As soon as I cut one to pieces and kick-scatter it, another comes from the side, or behind, or two at a time.

Swinging the chainsaw at a large, almost fully-formed Blackheart that rises at my side, I feel a clunk, and the blade sticks in heart. The chain breaks. It whips out. I'm a fraction of an inch from losing pieces of this husk.

The Blackheart rears up. I crouch and dodge to the side. I'm not quite far enough away. I hop to gain a few inches of clearance. Drawing the machete, I swing and slice, and first the limbs, then the heart of the large creature lies in pieces around me.

Where the hell is Jacob? Has this been his plan all along?

I take out two small creatures, not much more than a few shadows clinging to their dead hearts. They remind me of the Blackhearts from our side road a few hours before.

Has Jacob been waiting for me to wear myself out attacking, and then take me out from behind? Does he want to show the Director that he is the more worthy?

A swing, and I miss. The muscles are fatiguing. Is the Magic leaving me? A Blackheart lunges at my knee and wraps itself around my leg. The creature attaches itself and begins to tear at my jeans with the little serrated teeth that line the limbs. If I don't get it off, it'll make it past my pants and start tearing its way through my actual leg.

The awkward angle precludes any swinging, and now another Blackheart lunges and attaches itself to my left arm, wrapping itself around my wrist.

Panic rises with the gorge in my throat. The machete is a better weapon at a short distance, where I can get some leverage going. These things cling to me, and I can't get in there to pull them off.

Sparing a glance at the Director—she's not even looking at me. Me, her own creature. I rage inwardly at yet another disinterested God.

Where is Jacob?

The machete drops to the ground. I pull and tug at the creature on my leg, then the one on my arm. As if sensing that my capacity for lethal action has diminished, the rest of the creatures swarm my way.

The smell. Death and rotting meat swamp me in waves as the creatures wrap themselves around me. The eerie stillness provides an uncanny backdrop.

In the back of my memory, a void cracks open and yawns wide. Familiar territory. My memory snapshots fade slightly.

No! I will take them with me this time. All my beautiful families. Even my last, unfinished Jacob.

As the sunlight breaks in the east, the final Blackheart wraps itself across my face. The void completes itself and blackness swallows me whole.

The morning sun chases away the shadows and burns in my eyes, turning the back of my eyelids red in its glare.

Blinking, I prop myself up on my elbows. Parts of my husk ache in ways they've never ached before. The Moray Magic that binds us helps us to regenerate to a certain point, but I haven't tried pushing it this far before.

The midday sun beats down on the Director's home. It has an oddly cheering effect. It's still quiet; the only sound is the rustling through the trees and the occasional passing of a car or truck way out on the main road.

"Jacob?"

No answer.

I roll to my knees, pushing myself up off the ground. Ugh. Is this what getting old feels like? Count me out.

The vivid summer colors stand in stark contrast to the monochrome slaughterhouse that I'm standing in. Gore pools around my ankles, covering my shoes. Pieces of heart meat lie scattered in almost a whole layer across the grass. Much of it shows signs of being neatly quartered by blade or saw teeth—but the vast majority has been ripped into fine shreds by wendigo claws.

Of Jacob or the Director, there is not a sign.

I could go back to the truck. If Jacob hasn't made it there, I could grab the keys. Head on out. I've always wanted to see Montana. Who knows, at a distance from the Director, or maybe from her death, maybe this weird block on killing anything but Blackhearts will lift, and I can add to my memory snapshots. Maybe I'll start with Gettysburg Jacob.

The door opens.

Jacob stands there. He's wearing his wendigo face, and I immediately grope for my machete. I come up empty. He rolls his eyes—an interesting expression for a monster—and beckons me inside.

This day's been weird, and it's getting weirder. Looking around, I feel like I've stumbled onto the set of a Hollywood horror film during the day when they're setting up for a night shoot. Sunlight disinfects things like blood and monsters, and draws them from the realm of the supernatural into the world of the banal macabre.

I miss my old life.

Inside the house, I look to Jacob's lead. He heads upstairs, and I follow him into the kitchen. The gore is thick here as well, but in shades of black and red, instead of just the Blackhearts monochrome. What the hell happened?

"Where's the Director?" I ask.

Jacob waves a hand around vaguely. Ah. The red streaks. Understanding dawns.

"Well, that solves that problem, I guess." Weird. I would have thought that without her around, we'd just—I don't know. Fall apart?

The kitchen doesn't look like it was serving anything I'd like to eat. This must have been where the Director did her Magic. Mason jars filled with arcane ingredients line open cabinet shelves. A pot of something black and oily bubbles on the stove.

Jacob stands at the counter. Lined up neatly along the granite top stands a phalanx of dolls. They're shaped from clay, with little glass beads for eyes. Jacob picks one up. The dark hair and red glass beads look familiar.

Each doll sports one single, large tooth, extruding from their mouths. It's a comical effect, although some would probably run screaming from the sight. From the narrow spine and sharp point, it's obvious this tooth has come from Jacob's own collection.

My tongue darts toward the back of my mouth, playing around an empty place where a molar used to be. That same molar now resides in the doll Jacob hands me.

The poppet's dark green glass eyes gaze at me. I don't see the resemblance. I've always thought my eyes were more gray than green. With my thumb, I brush back the hair, brush the pads of my fingers over the eyes, the tooth. It's warm to the touch.

Some of the dolls are warm as well; others, missing their teeth, are corpse cold. That's where the "Moray" in Moray Magic comes from. Teeth like sharp knives in the dark.

Jacob tucks his doll into a pocket of his cargo pants.

There is a moment as we face each other across the kitchen, and I'm not sure which way things are going to go. I clench my fist. It's empty. My machete lies somewhere out on the front lawn.

Jacob bares his teeth. Bits of gore catch my attention. As the moment stretches out even longer, a globule of saliva collects and drips over the serrated bite of his lower jaw.

"My name is not Jacob."

And then he's gone.

Not-Jacob headed north. I went back south. Stopped by Gettysburg on the way, but there was no sign of my blonds. Probably for the best.

I've been on the road now for about four months. Winter was hard, but the old Ford came through. Yeah, Not-Jacob left me his ride. Guess he didn't need it where he was going.

I'm still not sure what I'm doing. The Director was as much a tyrant as anyone who holds others' lives in their hands, even a benevolent creator, who viewed us as tools in some obscure mission. Could be worse. Could have been better.

She'd been ready to move on to Paradox Echo, or so it seemed. The red splashes in the upstairs hadn't all come from her, and there'd been too many limbs scattered around. I'd had plenty of time to mull things over on the drive south. Not-Jacob saw the writing on the wall, a blood-red calligraphy that warned if the Director moved on from me, she would eventually tire of even her favorite creature. When we'd showed up together, she'd attacked us with the very things we were supposed to eliminate for her.

It doesn't make me mad, thinking about it. Nor surprised. It's not the first time I've faced hypocrisy and fear. Won't be the last, either, I think.

Still can't harm humans, but I've come close. Closer than before. Perhaps having control over my doll is loosening the Director's restrictions. Or maybe, her death is the reason I almost was able to reach out with my machete the last time I found a pair of perfectly matched father-daughter blonds.

I mostly stay off the highways, keeping to the side roads and hidden towns. Every once in a while, I find a nest and slice and scatter for old time's sake. And to relieve the itch. Until I can have the real thing.

Drove into a nice little town the other day. Stopped at the

diner. My waitress was a pretty young thing, blond hair, blue eyes, wearing some kid's high school ring on a chain around her neck. Apparently, her mama had passed, and she's been working in the restaurant with her papa, who owns the place.

He's young, too. Pleased to make my acquaintance.

We meet each other in the apartment above the diner, and he reaches for me. He is a good lover, and he tells me his name is Samuel. I call him Jacob. I reach for him.

I'm almost there.

SPIDERS

It was just a joke, barely a thought. They were on the playground again—the one they weren't supposed to play on. The jungle gym was old and rusted out in parts, but it was fine to play on, as long as you didn't push it on the swings.

There were two metal seats shaped like animals, a tiger and a seahorse, mounted on heavy-duty springs, so old you could barely get them to move. They kept talking about bringing a can of grease or something the next time they snuck out, but no one ever remembered.

Eloise, with the funny, old-fashioned name, had started hanging out with them at the playground. Or rather, they'd decided to defy town ordinance and parental warning and head down to the old park where they could each smoke half of the cigarette Bella'd stolen from her older brother's pack and play on the sets that were too young for them, and too old for anyone in the town that cared about their children's well-being. Eloise had been waiting there that first day, and they'd just kind of said hi and started including her in their conversations.

This was the old park, after all, as opposed to the New Glen Ridge Activity Field, all plastic and safety and shining off down the road. There was a soccer game going on over there today. People were wearing their masks over there.

"Hey, Eloise." Bella nodded to the girl, who was sitting on one of the faded red sections of the red and yellow merry-go-round. Most of the paint on the railings had worn off long ago, making it hot to the touch on a sunny day, but now the day had clouded over, and it wasn't too warm for Eloise to stretch her arms above her head, holding onto the railing, as she used one foot to push herself along.

"Woohoo!" Genevieve screeched and jumped on the merry-go-round, hopping up into the center and bending down to grab a railing on each side of the open space. "Let's see who gets sick first!"

Bella didn't take the bait. Instead, she sat down across from Eloise, leaning against a railing, mirroring the other girl's position. "What's up? You okay?"

Eloise shrugged, rubbing her back against the metal pole.

"UGH." Gennie flopped dramatically on her stomach between them, letting her head, shoulders and arms hang off the edge. "She *always* looks..." She trailed off and waved her arm up and down in Eloise's general direction, as if to indicate what the other girl was wearing.

It was her usual outfit. Black skirt, black tights—not pantyhose, tights—black turtleneck sweater, and saddle shoes. Bella didn't even know what they were called until she had described them to her mom, who'd seem surprised that they still made them, and that people still wore them. As always, Eloise's hair was parted in the middle and pulled back into two long, black braids. It wasn't that unusual of a hairstyle, not that Bella could tell. She wore hers cropped into a pixie cut, and Gennie had had her hair in locs since the seventh grade, so maybe it was what you did with long, straight hair.

Eloise rubbed her back against the metal pole again.

"Ha, you look like a bear in a nature video!" Gennie grinned. "All you need is some honey."

It would have sounded insulting coming from anyone else, but Gennie had a natural infectious laughter that she turned as easily against herself, and even Eloise cracked a grin at that one.

"Rawr," she said, making a halfhearted claw swipe with her curled fingers. "I want a nap."

Now that the ice was broken, as it always did, their conversation picked up. Eloise didn't talk as much as the others, but she would listen as they discussed kids at the school Eloise didn't go to, or promise to make a shopping date once their parents started letting them go places with other kids again.

Gennie stayed on her stomach, picking up rocks out of the overgrown weeds and chucking them towards the woods.

"UGH, we need to *go* somewhere." Gennie turned over and scootched herself up so she could lay on her back, resting her head on her hand. "I mean, how long is this going to—" She stopped and looked at her other hand. "Gross, what is *that*?"

The white, spherical object stuck to her hand, even when she turned her palm down.

"Oh, God, oh gross, it's on me, it won't get off." Gennie sat up and started waving her hand around.

"Stop."

Eloise grabbed Gennie's arm, arresting it in mid-flail.

"What is it?" Bella asked.

"Be careful." Eloise's voice sounded strange.

Gennie scrambled to a sitting position. "Hey, let go." She tried to wrench her arm away, but Eloise didn't let go.

"She is a mother," Eloise said. "A mother of all."

"Oh, come on." Bella rolled her eyes. "It's just a spider egg sac."

And without thinking, she leaned forward and plucked it off of Gennie's palm. Her friend scurried off the merry-go-round, dusting herself off in case any other unwanted visitors had hitched a ride.

"Bella, come on, let's go back to my place."

Bella wasn't listening. Instead, she stared at Eloise, who had fixed her gaze on the sac held gently in Bella's fingertips.

"Give them to me," she whispered.

Bella didn't know what she was thinking, it was more like a reflex, a joke that crossed her mind. "Sure, here they are!"

And she tossed the sac straight at Eloise's face.

It stuck to her cheek. At first, Gennie began to giggle, and Bella smiled, waiting for Eloise's reaction. But the other girl didn't jump up and down or get mad or cry.

Instead, the tiniest, thinnest line of black began to trickle out of the sac and make its way up Eloise's cheek.

"Oh ... oh my God, Eloise, I'm sorry." Bella ducked under the railing and slid off the merry-go-round, taking a step toward her.

Eloise held up a hand, and Bella stopped in her tracks.

The thin black line was joined by another, and then another, and finally a fourth line, all creeping and flowing up her cheeks. Two branched across her nose, seeking the orbs of her eyes. White orbs that the black lines crept into. And now, Bella could see the tiny, individual moving dots that made up those lines as they climbed into Eloise's eyes, creeping, crawling.

The white eyes that gradually filled to dark black pools, congealing, overflowing, seeking.

And now, Bella was backpedaling, Gennie was already running, the girls screaming, crying, stumbling away as Eloise stood, her skin bubbling with its dark carapace, growing, changing, stretching, bleeding.

"The mother..." Her mouth dripping with ichor, drooling around a set of pedipalps that waved, sensing. "I am ... the mother..."

And a mother must feed its young.

TANGLED

Under the waves, so cold and dark
Drifting along in the brine,
The little fish nudges the cold, blue skin
All wrapped in the soft, green vine.

Under the waves, so cold and dark
The abalones grow
Nestled amid the strange, strong limbs
As the currents shift to and fro.

Under the waves, so cold and dark
With face turned towards the sun—
But no rays can reach beneath the deep,
And the kelp is grasping, and tangled, and creeps
Around the legs to hold and to keep,
Its prize so cruelly won.

SHADOW POOL

ADINA'S HUSBAND LEFT SHORTLY AFTER THE WAVE BROKE HER against the rock wall. The darkness that reached up and tried to swallow her under left small shadows in the crags of her body, and while he might have been ready to go before, the knife in her hand sped his departure.

She remembered the sun across the water as they paddled their kayaks over an ocean that was restless with the previous night's storms. A pelican dropped down to the water a few yards in front of them, screaming its way down to the surface, backwinging as it paused above the wave, then furiously beat its way back to the heights, a string of brown kelp trailing from its massive beak.

The weather had been cool in the morning, but Adina had begun to sweat as she warmed under the fabric of her black wetsuit. She had paused to watch an otter, basking as it rode the waves, then paddled hurriedly to catch up with her husband. They had not smiled at each other in a long time, but on that particular day he had grinned widely as she attempted to maneuver the craft.

They had stopped at a large outcropping of rock. She hadn't wanted to get out of the kayak, so she held onto his as he climbed out and over the rock, scaring the seabirds into flight.

Their trip down the coast terminated at the cave, a small rocky outcropping open on both ends to allow the waves' passage. Her husband had smiled at her.

"Let's shoot it," he had said.

She had not even thought about refusing, but simply said, "After you."

He had nodded, grinned, and shot through with his paddle, riding up a wave, almost but not quite coming close to the low roof at the end of the cave—then down again, and he was safely through the passage. He waited for her in the sunlight on the other side in the small quiet pool beyond the mouth.

Adina had tried to follow suit but mistimed the wave. She caught one too high, and in trying to adjust, paddled too close to the wall. The ocean kayak scraped against a barely-submerged rock, and she was down in the vortex, spinning with the current.

Thinking about it now, her eyes blinked back against the salt that gathered in the corner of her eye.

She sliced the tomato thin. The knife slid cleanly through the skin, separating the walls and pulp until the neat partitions fell precisely upon the cutting board. Each rise and fall of the blade left a fresh scar on the wooden surface.

There was nothing unfitting, nothing unusual, she thought. It happened that she was underwater for a time, then she was above the surface. She had returned with a smile, her face radiant, squinting towards the sun. She did not understand this need to put a deadline on anxiety, the necessity for fear.

All her husband's dread had sucked out her own. Looking back, it seemed it had always been that way—another's horror —anxiety so stark against the bleach of her own psyche. She wondered about their fear, their insistence that she feel what they expected, even though she never could.

Adina was drawn to strong emotions; the closest she came to feeling something besides the even, gray void was curiosity. She had once stood in the road at the age of eight, smiling and holding her hands out to the oversized red SUV that screeched to a halt bare inches from her small frame. The driver, who, minutes before, had been texting her boss, had looked up in time to keep from running Adina into the pavement. The woman had wet herself and was embarrassed to get out of the car, her face blanched white under the crippling latent shock of what had almost happened.

When Adina broke her leg at the age of fifteen, she suffered her mother to hold her close, not for comfort, but to see if she could somehow borrow those emotions that sprang so readily up in others. She'd opened her mouth, panting, as if she might somehow taste them.

All she tasted these days was salt. It had been in her eyes and nose and ears under the water, a white, blind cave that curled around her, spinning her in its embrace.

The memory played with her sense of time, packing eternity into a few brief seconds. Adina remembered the tug on her ankle from the kayak leash, then the fleeting, shadowy pressure that crushed her skin and pierced her pores, seeking the dark hollows of her body. She had felt—or thought she had felt—something questing, thrusting, and finally erupting within her as she struggled for the surface.

She had exploded through the skin of the water, rippling towards the inlet that calmed beyond the cave opening. Adina had opened her eyes to the worry and fear rising in her husband's face.

Adina stood, motionless, the knife resting blade-down on the cutting board. She came out of her thoughts slowly, the red fruit coming back into focus as she returned her gaze to the task at hand.

She lifted the cutting board and scraped the red chunks into a large green bowl. Setting bowl and board back on the table, she carefully selected another tomato—large, ripe, smelling of vines. She lifted it to her nose and breathed deep, reveling in the salt-tinged scent of summer.

Adina raised the knife again. A glob of red pulp slid down the blade, dripped past the knuckles of her hand. She felt it drop on her bare foot.

Holding her sundress out of the way, pressing it against her protruding belly, she tried to dab at the pulp with a paper towel. The contours of her body defeated her. She straightened back up, one hand holding her lower back. She licked the juice from her finger and paused. She felt something shift and roll, spreading limbs against the watery darkness.

The wave passed, and Adina placed the knife against the tomato and sliced it into narrow pieces. The pulp on her foot slid onto the floor and began to dry. It stung the scab across the knuckles of her toes.

When she came up from the water, she was bleeding—head, shoulder, and the top of her foot. She had hit, scraped, and been dragged along the rough rock of the cave wall. Another pain came without bleeding.

Her husband stayed with her three months after the accident. She was three months pregnant, but she thought he knew the child wasn't his. It might not even be properly called hers.

She paused, laying a palm against her swollen belly, felt momentarily lightheaded. It passed.

Adina placed the knife against the skin of the tomato and cut another slice. A sharp pain from her abdomen twisted the knife in her hand, and she gasped and dropped the fruit. The juice splattered across her naked foot, mingling with the scar that still oozed wetly. The tomato half-rolled and came to a rest.

She bent against the cramping that went on for a short eternity. It was different from the other pains that had been coming with greater frequency and intensity the past week. One final scrape and the pain stopped abruptly. Adina waited a moment and bent to retrieve the tomato.

It stuck momentarily to the floor, the spreading red pool already drying into a tacky gum. Adina gazed dispassionately at the ruined fruit, then at the body propped against the cabinets. Already, the skin had assumed a waxen pale aspect, and the first bruises of postmortem lividity appeared like small purple flowers where buttocks, thighs, calves and heels pressed against the floor. Adina tossed the tomato into the sink. She unclasped and reclasped her hand around the knife handle. Her shoulders ached with the effort of slicing through the muscle under the skin.

The salad bowl was half filled with cucumbers and tomatoes, lightly salted, with a few crumbles of feta cheese across the top. She would wait until right before she served it to add the final dressing. She covered it and put it into the refrigerator.

The chicken was almost ready to go in the oven. Arranged neatly in a shallow casserole dish, she had minced onions, garlic and mushrooms and topped it off with salt, pepper and rosemary. She covered the dish with aluminum foil, rested it on top of the range, and turned the oven to 375 degrees to preheat. If she timed it right, it would be baked through just when he walked in the door.

Her work in the kitchen done, Adina dispensed herself a glass of water from the tap, sprinkled it copiously with salt, and wandered into the living room. Her feet tacked slightly on the kitchen linoleum, and she paused at the edge of the carpet. She wiped her feet, leaving faint brown stains.

The apartment was small—front door opening into the living room, a single bedroom, small bathroom, and the kitchen. The living room showed hardly a sign of its previous occupant. No pictures, no magazines open to the last article read. A few decorations littered the walls, of the sort single women without memories bought at a generic box store. There was nothing of interest there.

The bedroom was neat and contained. Adina paused in the door. Finally, one scent permeated past the omnipresent brine. She breathed deeply, catching after the hints of his cologne, its presence stronger here than in the home he used to live in. Every time she caught a fleeting whiff, she almost felt something, something that might have been loss.

Or maybe anger. She couldn't hold on to it long enough to tell.

The pain came again, this time lower, sharper. It held her in its grasp longer. She clenched her hands, realized she still carried the knife in her other hand. It passed. Adina straightened. She took a sip of the saltened water and wiped her mouth with the back of her hand. It was time to put the chicken in the oven.

The smell of garlic and chicken in its own juices permeated the small kitchen. Adina turned the oven to low and left the foil over the casserole dish so the meat wouldn't dry out. She set two places on the table, opening several cabinets and drawers until she found the ones containing dishes, wine glasses, napkins, silverware. She added two mismatched candlesticks she found in a drawer, placing the salad between them.

Adina set her water glass down in front of one of the places. She noted the place where her thumb had left a smudged print and bent forward to polish it with her napkin. Her back twinged. The loud buzz of the doorbell, followed by the jangling of the key in the lock, interrupted her preparations.

He was as handsome as she remembered. He had grown a beard—that was different—a neatly-trimmed goatee. It was slightly darker than his blonde hair. His eyes were lighter than her memory, the sunlight from the window next to the door brightening them.

"Adina?" he asked. "What are you doing here?"

He stepped into the little foyer, overcoat over one arm, briefcase in the other. He held his keys in his hand, forgetting to drop them on the little table against the wall. He took another step, stopped short at the stains her feet had left on the carpet.

"What's going on?" he asked.

"Marco," she said. "Dinner's just finished."

"What the hell is going on?" This time he yelled, the words half-demanding, half-already knowing, not wanting to know.

She crumpled.

The pain came again, and she sank back into the chair. The knife clattered out of her hand.

"What did you do?" he asked, his voice little more than a whisper.

He stepped toward her, stopping as he caught sight of the bloodstains on the carpet, left from her bare feet. "What have you done?"

He dropped his overcoat and briefcase on the ground, sprinting to the bedroom. She heard the pounding footsteps stop short, listened as he called his girlfriend's name, the panic in the sound rising in her ears like the crashing of the tide.

Marco came back down the hall, not running this time, trying to maintain his composure. Adina sat in the chair, calm, composed. She shuddered as another pain rippled through her body.

"Where is she?" he asked. "What did you with her?"

"I made you dinner." A tear gathered at the corner of Adina's eye, rolled down her cheek along the shining path. She licked it away. "Everything's ready."

Marco backed away from her, shaking his head. He was sweating. She had turned off the air conditioner and moisture had begun to pool under his armpits and bead on his forehead.

He staggered and half-tripped into the kitchen. Adina

heard a scream, a frantic thing that ended in a low-pitched moan. She licked her lips against the salt that gathered at the corner of her mouth. There was some small taste there. She found it oddly comforting.

Her husband stumbled back into the room, panic on his face. He lurched toward her, menacing, and she felt a small something, maybe even a moment of what could be called fear. But then his face crumpled, and he collapsed, crawling towards her. He clasped her about the legs.

"Why?" he asked, clutching her in an embrace not unlike a child's. "Why did you come here? Why did you do this?"

Adina reached down and patted him on the head.

"I'm leaving now," she said.

He clutched her more tightly, as if to try to stop her. She moved the chair away and knelt down. Her belly made the posture awkward, but she gathered him to her, and he rested against the swell of her side.

Another ripping pain crashed through her. This one was the most intense yet, and she clasped him tightly against her stomach so he could feel the motion like a current running through her.

"It's coming," she said.

He dropped his hands, drawing back, scrambling back on hands and knees to get away from her.

"You have to go to the hospital," he said. "I have to call the police. I have to—"

He broke off, searching for his phone, pawing the pockets of his overcoat. He stopped and stood very still as he felt the keen, cool edge of the knife on his throat. Adina stood over him, the calm, stoic expression on her face belying the determination in her stance as she pressed the blade against his skin.

"It was necessary," she said. He struggled against her. His movements weakened, subsided.

"Why?" The word stood between them, heavy in the late summer sun, drifting through the silence of the dwelling.

She brought her fingers to her mouth, tasting once again the faint coppery salt of the sacrifice. Adina had once thought she felt something for this man at her feet, who sat frozen in the path of the knife. And it was that latent, fast-forgotten hope that kept him from falling under it. His girlfriend appeased the compulsion growing in his ex-wife's belly.

"I have to go now," she said, and she went, locking the door safely behind her.

* * *

The streets of the tiny California beach town were almost deserted in the fading afternoon. The pavement was covered in a fine mist of gravel near the edges, and she flinched as she set her bare feet down. The sun had warmed the black tar until it almost hurt. She stepped gingerly, wincing as she made her way along.

A red pickup truck with two surfboards in the back rolled slowly up the street towards her, on its way back from the small stretch of sand at the bottom of the hill. Many of the local surfers and kayakers used the tiny beach as a jumping off point into the great western ocean. It was rarely crowded, and the long set of stairs to get to the beach ensured that most tourists would eschew the location in favor of a more popular, easier-to-access coastline. Adina knew the spot. She had been there before.

The truck slowed as the driver caught sight of her picking her way down the street. He was older, a shock of gray hair mussed by wind and waves falling over his tanned face.

"Ma'am, are you all right?" he asked out of the open window.

Adina stopped walking and turned slowly to face him. "Yes, I'm fine. I have to go."

"Are you sure?" he asked, and put the car in neutral, pulling up on the brake. He reached outside of the window and grasped the handle, as if to open the door. It was an old truck.

"I'm fine," she said. "Please go."

The point of the knife in his face changed his mind. He threw up his hands.

"No worries," he said. "You got someplace to go, I can see."

Satisfied, she withdrew the knife and continued walking. He watched her go in his driver's side mirror. He didn't have a cell phone to call the cops—you didn't need one on the waves —so he jerked the shift lever into first gear and peeled out toward home. Just one more weird day on the California coast.

The water was warm, although the sun sat even closer to the horizon. The pains in Adina's abdomen came quickly now, without relief, as they relentlessly twisted her body in on itself. The waves were dying down, tranquility spreading across the sea.

She paused halfway down the stairs, catching herself as the hardest contraction rolled through, crashing her against the metal railing, forcing her to hang on to the supports and struts so as not to fall to the soft sand below. She clasped her arms protectively around herself.

The pressure between her thighs built up. She waited, trying to breathe, until the wave subsided. Her body paused, a momentary retreat in the battle, leaving her gasping. Something in her knew the final moment was near.

It was hard to walk on the sand. It rolled beneath her, her feet and ankles sinking deep into the large grains. Shards of shells sliced the bottoms of her feet, leaving tiny glints of salty red on their edges. She did not care—was beyond caring—where she stepped, and the rolling edge of the next subsiding wave reached up to caress her wounds with its salty embrace.

She stood in the waves up to her calves, buffeted by their incoming, retreating rolls, feeling her body responding, shifting, assuming the rhythm of the surf. Deep within her, she remembered the taste of salt and meat on her tongue, the pieces of sacrifice she had taken into her body, to feed life in its final quest to be born.

And then Adina was out past the surf, beyond the rollers that sought the land, caught in the current returning to the sea. The sounds of the water crashing against the coast became muted; she lost them in her senses, supplanted by the deep, vibrant keening arising from the deep.

The sound grew in pitch and intensity, snaking through the waves, wrapping around her legs and lower body, caressing her back as she bent in agony, holding her head above the surface. She looked around in eyes gone blurry and caked with salt. She tried to reach out for something, anything, but there was nothing to hold onto in the water.

The current lifted her from the bottom of the ocean, the slick mud and vegetation under her feet. She felt her body raised and opened, the sun sending its red streaks across her limbs, exposed to the air. Her sundress was ripped, rent from the pressures tearing her apart, and the limbs that twisted around her from the depths. She was bleeding now, the red mingling with the sun.

The red ball paused on the edge of the horizon, hovering

on the edge of being and nonbeing—it sank low, vanishing with a brilliant green flash that pierced her through. She screamed, the sound blending with the drone from the creature below her, who twined her in its embrace, seeking her and finding her through the currents threading the seas. She felt whole and broken, torn apart and reeling, as the life within her finally pushed its way into the open sea.

Adina floated, drifting, the breakers taking her farther from the shore with the curious current that swimmers and surfers in that area knew to be dangerous for its arbitrary, unpredictable habit of drowning those who were caught in its casual grasp. She missed the pressure that used to be within her, the limbs that twined around her, the feeling of almost feeling that had been hers when the creature had been growing in her. The sky was darkening, and she started to feel the cold deep under her skin.

The salt in the water now nauseated her. Her head rested on the surface, half-submerged. Every so often, a small whitecap would break over her, and she would taste salt and seawater and undercurrents of ocean life.

She thought she heard the vibrations again, the murmur growing louder, and she welcomed the return of her progeny. A larger, darker shape swam by its side, and they drew near her, nudging and nestling against her in the gentle sea.

The first sensation of teeth on her ankle was not unpleasant. The sharp pain broke the skin, but Adina welcomed it as a nursing mother welcomes the bite of her child's teeth on her breast.

Another bite came, this one on her inner thigh, joined by another on her arm, another on her stomach. A multitude of questing, hungry mouths came, and she fell under their onslaught. She arched her back, the pain mixing with pleasure as she drifted away, falling to pieces across the waves, consumed by the life that had once grown within her.

A vision came of the stars, their light bright across the tips of the water. Adina sank deeper, into water and into nothingness. She fell, grasping toward feeling, finally feeling. Not terror, not pain, not panic—

Complete.

IRONFAE

I WAS FIDDLING WITH MY BANK CARD WHEN I SAW THE clockwork girl. She watched, eyes spinning in steel and flashes from the sirens that went by. I waited until the blue sparks faded, then pulled out my Leatherman to jimmy the card out.

The steel blade sprang back from the slot with a spark that reminded me of iron and flint, biting deep into the web of my thumb and forefinger. I cursed and looked back to see if the girl was still there, but she had disappeared. Or it could have been a mirage. I had been up for a straight thirty-six hours, and the money was meant for a caffeine binge to fuel at least another twenty-four.

The deserted street stretched out and a swirl of crumpled newspaper caught my eye. She was maybe a stray, she was maybe my imagination. She was maybe too many comic book frames populated with ink-spattered, time-tocking hobgoblins.

I slipped my multitool back in my jacket. It sat there, comforting cold iron in my pocket. My brain was still wired with pixelated steam; my watch had stopped shortly after my second midnight. I looked around, checking the emptiness of the street. I had been followed home once before, and had met that visitor with Iron. So I was more cautious these days when visited by clockwork girls in the alley.

She was sitting on the fence in front of my building. This was a feat. When I left on my aborted coffee run, the wrought-iron sprouted forbidden spears of do-not-enter. Those high thorns were now intricate leaves that faintly shone under the yellow street light. I closed my eyes and opened them again, catching a whisper of black-shining movement in the shadow.

Ticking clocked in my ear, so loudly I looked around expectantly. I realized my watch had started under her gaze. I brought it to my ear, then let my hand fall back to my pocket.

"I have six days left," I said. "That was the deal."

She cocked her head to one side, then shrugged her thin shoulders. I heard a faint creak of gears.

"I like it better this way," she said, blinking back early-morning drizzle.

I raised my eyebrow. "That's supposed to be iron you're sitting on."

She smiled a toothy smile of tick-tock amusement. I swore I saw something metallic gleam before her lips returned to thin, wry lines.

"Will you invite me in?"

Or what? I wanted to ask. Or she might rust?

"What do you want?"

"I need a portrait."

"I don't do portraits anymore." Not for people, not for money, and certainly not for clockwork hooligans who follow me back from the ATM.

She giggled a sound that sounded like an old Ford changing gears.

"Of course you will." The breath steamed from her certainty.

"And why is that?"

"Because I can offer you far more than Iron for your protection."

And so she creaked and tocked her way up the flight of stairs to my tiny studio, where my solitary clock kept watch over the darkroom. She perched her thin steel frame on a stool.

My portraits are not so much frames and lighting as they are silver and time. The light from the outside drenched the studio. In the daylight, it was calm and reassuring and bathed my subjects in memories of summer and ice cream and lost moments of forgotten joy.

The night from the outside carries a weird silver, and it was trying to capture the iron darkness that first led me to set my antique Yashica on a tripod and open up the shutter all the way, waiting to see what the moon would bring to the frame.

The clockwork girl was not the first Fae to appear in shadows of nitrate.

"Should I smile?" she asked.

I made a last adjustment to the camera. It was a quick set-up, and I wanted her gone.

"It's your portrait," I said.

She straightened on the stool, moonlight coppering the wisps of wire that escaped her knit hat. She was dressed, not in rags, but in suggestions of linen and steel.

I burned twenty-four frames at the sedate pace of the minute hand, until the barest suggestion of the end of night sank the moon behind the cityscape. As I worked, she told me a story. Not in so many words, but in the clock-ticking poses and smiling hints of rhyme behind her visage.

I would have thought time had stopped, and that she had something to do with it, but then the clock—the real one, the solitary one on the wall—chimed its reality.

"I have caught you time," said the clockwork girl as she stood on the wooden floor planks.

I blinked against the sudden light. Straightening, I felt a twinge in my back, reminders of mortality fast approaching.

She laughed. "I have wrought you such protections as no one will think to challenge."

Confused, I bent my head to winding the film back into its spool.

The momentary dawn darkened, and the clock paused in its cyclic journey. It had been carving slices away from me since the last portrait I had captured.

Two weeks ago, I accidentally caught a Demonfae as she capered along the brownstone, seeking playthings from the shadows. I had transgressed arcane, forgotten rules that endured even through the fading of them from awareness. For my penance, I was bereft of time and memory.

"The black dog has been turned back," said the Iron Queen. "I have sent it on its clockwork way."

I found myself on my knees, light streaming past the window, casting a harsh shadow from the stool a few feet from the window.

My camera stood on its tripod, sole witness to my sacrifice and reprieve. The film burned through the silver.

I left the portrait, the best of the roll, firmly tamped into the Iron wroughtwork. I didn't stay to keep watch, but I suspect it was neither blown away by the wind nor borrowed by a curious stranger, but rather plucked carefully out of the Iron by long, fragile, clockwork fingers.

THE CARNIVAL GHOST

"HE WAITS, STANDING IN THE SHADOWS, HIDING THE HORRIBLE burns on his face."

Pierrette kept her voice low and throaty, rasping a little as the glow of the oil lamps flickered over the grease paint on her face. The crowd of townie kids sat entranced, listening with a mixture of awe and rapture that enveloped even the older boys.

"So, when you're traveling back home after the show, run fast and don't look behind you." She pitched her voice even lower. "For the Carnival Ghost could be following in the shadows ... close ... behind..."

"*YOU!*"

The apparition leapt from behind the curtain, waving its limbs and shrieking. Children screamed, cried, and scrambled to escape the storytelling tent. One small girl fell and couldn't get up again. Pierrette, prepared for this occurrence, snatched her up. Holding her close, she murmured, "Don't fret, *ma petite,* it's just a man in a silly disguise."

Jacques grinned and lifted the white half-mask to reveal a

young, unlined face not much older than the teenage boys who'd sat listening to the story.

"Tell Jacques, he's a bad Carnival Ghost to frighten you like that!" Pierrette wiped the girl's tears and shook her finger at Jacques. The girl smiled and ducked her head into Pierrette's shoulder.

"Louise!" A woman in her twenties poked her head in to the tent, then rushed to take the little girl, who reached for her with a cry of "*Mamá!*"

Pierrette's wistful gaze followed them out of the tent, the bells on her collar drooping with a sad little jingle as she turned to glare at the other clown. "Jacques, you are terrible. You must not be so ... *enthusiastic* around the smaller children."

Jacques laughed and blew her a kiss. "They come to the carnival to see a show. How could I leave without giving them their money's worth?" His mouth twisted. "Or their *Papá's* money's worth." He flicked one of the bells on her shoulders and bowed, mockingly. "*Bonne nuit, mon petit Pierrot.* Don't let the Carnival Ghost haunt you!"

The spectre, fondly known as the Carnival Ghost, was an old legend half-believed by even the younger, more modern members of *Le Cirque de la Lune*. But his was not that shadow that haunted Pierrette like a black-winged bird, hovering over her shoulder just out of eyesight. Instead, the images took the form of her mother, father, and older brothers, darkened and smudged, as if seen in an old mirror.

What Pierrette wouldn't have given to have run to her *Mamá* like the little girl in the sideshow. But as always, her own memories ended in a wall of thick black smoke, the red flames flickering along the bottom, her own cries for her mother unanswered.

With the scent of smoke still playing around her nostrils, Pierrette wiped the remnants of greasepaint from her face and doused the lamp at the dressing table she shared with the other girls. She wasn't sure exactly what time it was, but there were a few hours of darkness left. The show had ended hours ago, and even as late as carny folk stayed up, everyone would now be asleep.

As she did every night, Pierrette crept from the wagon and softly padded through the darkness to the main tent. She lifted the flap and paused just inside the canvas walls.

"Hello?" Her whisper faded into the vast, dark space. "Madame?"

A flapping movement above her caused her to jump. A soft chirrup and a re-settling of wings reassured her that she had only disturbed a pair of barn swallows. They bobbed their heads as they tucked them back under their wings, settling in for the night on the tightrope that stretched across the empty space.

"Ah, to be a bird," the lightly accented voice murmured behind Pierrette. "Always fluttering, always so high above."

Pierrette smiled, but her words held a bitter note. "I could only dream of such flight." She turned to face the other woman who had materialized behind her.

"Perhaps," the woman said. "But tonight, is no time for dreams. Is time for work."

"Yes, Madame."

A soft whickering greeted Pierrette as the woman stepped forward, leading a powerful gray gelding behind her. The horse, familiar with the routine, nuzzled Pierrette's shoulder as she took the bridle reins from Madame.

Pierrette took a breath to center and calm. Her horse took

his cue from her, and it would never do to perform in a state of impatience or agitation.

Her horse? Pierrette grinned. The gray was one of many who performed in the carnival's equestrian shows. She didn't know how Madame coaxed him away from his fellows without him raising an alarm, or how the woman dwelled undetected in the carnival's shadows, but perhaps ghosts had their methods, and she did not care to inquire too closely, lest her benefactor fade with the morning camp smoke.

Pierrette unsnapped the reins from the bridle and laid them carefully to the side nearest Madame. As always, the woman wore a scarf of white silk to cover half her face. A network of scars radiated down her chin, the deepest extending across her throat. Pierrette did not know where the scars had come from, but she had never heard Madame speak above a harsh whisper thanks to them.

"Tonight," Madame said. "I think you are ready to fly."

"Yes, Madame."

Pierrette slapped the horse gently on the shoulder. "*Allez!*"

The gray started trotting in a circle around the ring. Pierrette flexed and waited as he started back around toward her. Taking a few short steps, she launched herself in a double forward flip, at the end of which she landed parallel to the horse. Taking another step, she leaped into the air, alighting gently yet firmly on the horse's back.

The wind catches in her hair, but now Pierrette is three years old. Under a sunny sky, she giggles as her stubby toddler feet inch along the double rope strung low between two stakes. The grass in the open field is just high enough to tickle the bottoms of her toes as she makes it all the way to the other side, turning triumphantly to make sure her parents and older brothers have seen what she's done.

As she turns, the sky fades and darkens. A roaring sound swells until it deafens her. She claps tiny hands over her ears and screams, but the wave of thunder drowns out her cries.

"*Mamá! Papá!* Claude! Jean!"

Now six years old, Pierrette runs from tent to tent, seeking a hiding place to protect her from the unwanted attentions of the other carny brats. She is an easy target in this rundown sideshow—brought to the carnival by an alcoholic uncle who soon expired and left her in the care of disinterested adults who measured members by how much money they could bring in.

Pierrette ducks under the flap of a tent. She has found them—the tightrope acrobats! What luck! With beauty and grace, they soar and dance on the ropes high above, bowing and turning as they move confidently through the air. On the ground, another little girl practices on a low-strung double rope. Pierrette smiles and runs to her. She remembers this! Perhaps they will let her on the rope and she can show them she, too, is a tightrope acrobat.

"Get out of here!" The little girl punctuates her words with a sharp shove. Pierrette falls, twisting her ankle beneath her. The little girl laughs. "Get out, you stupid clown."

Pierrette cries, not having learned yet that tears are naught but water, and nothing will dry them except the hem of her own ragged skirt.

Now she is eight, wiser and harder, practicing her part of the clown act with sad tears that have been painted on her cheek. No longer do any real ones ever breach her eyelids. Instead, she sings and dances and suffers the brunt of the other clowns' jokes.

When the show is over, she hides, finding small nooks and crannies where questing, mocking carnies can never find her. Pierrette finds comfort in the early-morning darkness, when she can practice the rudimentary acrobatics far from any who would seek to push her or ridicule her rusty ambitions.

It is there, under the darkness of the big tent, where Pierrette practices handstands along the narrow rim of the ring, that *Madame le Fantome*, the Carnival Ghost, first speaks to her.

"Will you dance for me?" she whispers to Pierrette. "Will you spring for me, my angel?"

Pierrette is an eager pupil, and she quickly learns the steps Madame shows her, ones the older woman once danced on the Paris stage, until seduced by one man who lived in the night, and betrayed by another who took his place. But she is too young to understand.

At ten years of age, Pierrette is an accomplished acrobat, although the only witness to her perfect flips and pirouettes is an old woman who wears a silk scarf to hide her face. The Carnival Ghost pushes Pierrette to learn, to practice, to not give up. She is harsh, but knowledgeable of a great many things. Pierrette laughs now, as she listens to the whispered tales shared over campfires and told in stories to small children. *If you only knew!*

One night, Pierrette has another set of questions for the Ghost. One that centers around the changes in herself, and her body. Questions that she would ask her mother, needing another woman to explain what is happening to her. The Ghost saddens, draws her close. There are no acrobatics that night, only soft comforting in the moonlight that drifts in like smoke.

———

Four years of training have strengthened Pierrette's limbs into coiled springs. She dances atop the thundering gray, one moment standing on her hands as he circuits the ring, the next plucking a rope out of the air and skipping along his back.

She leaps and pirouettes, springing from the horse to the ground and up again. Pierrette and the gray caper around the ring in another circle, picking up speed. They run faster and faster until it seems they must surely fly, crashing, out of the ring.

At the peak of the rush, the gray screeches to halt, rearing high, hooves in the air. Pierrette flies off his back, in what seems like a terrible accident—until she flips three somersaults in the air and lands in the soft sand beside him.

Together, Pierrette and the gray take a bow. She dips at the waist; the gray extends his right foreleg. Where a tumultuous assault of applause should occur, there is instead total silence.

———

Pierrette breathed hard, trying to control her pounding heart and heaving sighs. Blood thundered in her ears. Beside her, the gray shivered and whinnied.

Not hearing anything, Pierrette risked a quick glance up. Madame stared at her, her gaze thoughtful.

"Is Madame ... pleased?"

The woman tucked an iron-gray strand of hair back under her silk scarf. Slowly, she smiled, the facial gesture marred by the sideways pull of the muscles hidden under the mask.

"Madame is pleased." She wiped a tear that clung to a lash.

Pierrette stood, stunned. She had never thought that Madame could portray such naked emotion. And yet, had she, too, not wanted to cry as she flew around the ring? For once, she wished she could cry tears other than paint.

"Thank you, Madame."

Pierrette awoke to screams and running feet. Drowsily, she poked her head out of the wagon.

Jacques, darting by, paused to gesture at her. "Come, Pierrette." He gestured again, impatient. "Come! They're saying Mademoiselle Rue has been murdered by the Carnival Ghost."

Pierrette forgot everything and ran after him in her bare feet, robe flying about her. She joined a rush of the other folk as they gathered like storm clouds around the center ring of the big tent.

There, before her, lay the broken doll body of the Mademoiselle Catelyn Rue, the female member of the Rue Riders, the family who performed such stunning equestrian feats for the circus.

"What happened?" Jacques had jostled his way to Pierrette's side. She had snuck and wriggled herself to the front of the crowd.

"They're saying she fell." Pierrette's voice was flat and unhorrified.

"From the tightrope?" Jacques' astonishment was reflected in his voice. "But how did ... *quelle horreur...*"

Pierrette left his question unanswered, but she knew what had happened. In fact, whispers of "the Carnival Ghost" and "*Madame le Fantome*" traded freely among the folk gathered behind her.

A sharp, muttered conversation in front of her drew her attention, and she tuned Jacques out.

"This will ruin us if it gets out." The tall man with the vest over his pajamas spoke to a short, barrel-chested man with spectacles. "We need a replacement."

"*Oui*, but where will we find one?" The ringmaster, for it was he, answered the owner of the carnival. "The Rues will just have to go on minus one for tonight's show."

"I can do it."

Pierrette's statement was lost in a general murmur, so she spoke up again, louder. "I can do it, *messieurs*. I can do the trick riding." They fixed confused, dismissive glances on her, but she met them with confidence. "I can show you."

Jacques stared at Pierrette, silently demanding answers, but she did not mind. In front of them, the body of the small female rider also remained mute. The dead do not give up their secrets.

The crowd packed into the huge tent always made the space seem smaller than it was. The rings stretched out before her. At Pierrette's side, the familiar gray whinnied, waiting for his cue.

The music swelled. The ringmaster nodded in her direction. After seeing her perform, there had been no question that she should take Mademoiselle Rue's place. Especially, and this was only whispered where the shadows couldn't hear, since she now had the Carnival Ghost as a patron. Pierrette raised her hand.

Bringing her arm down, she brushed the horse's shoulder. The gray gelding leaped up, prancing on his hind legs and pawing the air. Falling to the ground, he pivoted and knelt before her.

The crowd clapped its anticipation. In the front row, a small girl gripped her parents' hands, leaning forward, eyes aglow under the lights.

Pierrette gathered herself, sparing one final thought to the Carnival Ghost, whose macabre patronage had cleared her this spot on the stage.

"Thank you, Madame Daaé," she whispered. "*Merci, Mamá.*"

And with that, she leapt into the air, taking flight.

PIERCED MONARCH

THE POETS DESCRIBED IT AS A RATTLE, BUT HE FELT IT MORE AS A shirr of butterfly wings in the front of his throat, as they pelter-patted against the orange walls with their unmistakable dust of death.

The prophet had written words (numb, syllabic challenges —he had put that prophet to death and anonymity) describing the challenges of threading the needle of redemption. A woman's slip, the tailor mends, and sweet silence is introduced with the pricking of a new gown. The thorns, hidden in the new crown, place added emphasis on the final blow.

If death, he mused, is like sleeping, in a grimace mocking rest, why then must my eyes remain open, fixed on fantasies of perfidy and change? Is this the hand that moved regiments like chess pieces across quilted battlefields of northern marches? Are these the woven braids, each enemy killed in combat, that ornate the feared visage of royal countenance? Counter light, glaring, beneath roil framed shadows of loyalty.

And the dying regent summoned daggers, utilitarian

blades, plunging them in the recesses of his arms. Blood seeped, slowing, freed of the urgency of vascular rhythm. The fading echoes were shadows and light on falling wings.

———

Inspired by the painting "Pierced Monarch" by Marrus.

THE TERRIBLE, VAST PYRE OF CHIEF
MACHINIST KIRLISOVEYITCH

The intricacies of grief
Transwhelmed this moment
Into the monochromed gilt of clockwork landscape,
Ticking time in heartbeats
Unsteady under copper clouds
Held bursting in these
Lungs of red iron chains.

THE KILLING TIME BEGAN AGAIN AS THE CLOCKWORK BEAR AWOKE
in his mountain of rough iron. The knowledge seeped into the
city, subsuming the rhythm of industry and speech into the
barely heard heartbeat of clock-step marching.

"The *paradematnyes* are massing again." The woman in the
red dress pronounced the second syllable with the affected
long "a" that was all the rage these days among the upper
classes, comprised of those with enough money to do nothing
inside the winter walls of steam and steel.

She stepped back from the window as her breath frosted thick on the pane.

The man in the black suit looked up from his newspaper. Sighing, she paled against the curtains, drawing them back across the glass. He narrowed his eyes at the affectation. It glared, garish and obvious, against the images holding his mind in thrall.

Kirlisoveyitch was dead.

It looked like he had punched his own ticket. It happened. The days of darkness sometimes weighed heavily on the soul, and the fires lit in the great caverns of steel could not warm the mind as they did flesh and metal.

Still, the news came as a surprise and would no doubt cause great disconcertment in the camps. He folded the newspaper and placed it into his leather satchel, tying the clasp with a thin piece of twine. The copper buckle had broken years ago, and he had not bothered to replace it.

"Karl," the woman said. "Be careful."

He nodded without replying. Swirling his greatcoat about him, he settled it on his shoulders and pulled the tall fur hat snugly over his ears.

The gas in the streetlights flickered and guttered as he made his way through the half-lit streets. At this early time of night, commotion was not unusual, but the snow that continued to fall made it unlikely. Still, if the massing continued, he expected his journey would be delayed by half as long as it took the *Korolmatnyes* to quell the careful demonstration.

The long street with its well-kempt rows of brick encased in wrought iron finally ended, the cobblestones giving way to the slush-encrusted dirt of a wide parade square illuminated by a bonfire encased in a giant copper furnace. The buildings surrounding the square hunched in the darkness, their windows illuminated every so often by sparks of reflection that thrust their way through the gloom and smoke that over-hung the parade field.

Lined in gleaming ranks before the fire, three-meter tall *paradematnyes* waited in their dominant copper lines. Snowflakes brushed the air around them, fading into water and drizzle in the heat thrown off by the metal giants.

Something in his stride kept the few human observers from straying too near his steps. Their presence was a redundancy, a simple failsafe, and they sensed in his stride a subtle danger to their careful chaos.

"Good evening, Comrade Engineer."

He was unwilling to slow his steps, but the man's voice held exactly the right mix of address and deference. The man grasped his fur-lined uniform cap, lifting it exactly the right distance from his head. His other hand grasped a small wooden box.

"Good evening, Maestro," he replied, nodding his head.

"Yuri," the man said, replacing his capeau. "Maestro Yuri."

"Impressive display."

"Thank you." Maestro Yuri bobbed his head. "Will you be observing the demonstration?"

"Regretfully, no," Karl said, offering no further explanation.

The Maestro bobbed his head again and gave a short bow. He turned back to the square. Flipping open his box, he waited for his control gears to emerge. He grabbed the control, insulated in its rubber tube, and shifted it into position. Nodding to his fellow Controllers positioned at the corners of the square, the Maestro pressed a small, tear-shaped button.

Behind him, Karl heard the muffled roar of lubricated joints and metal meeting the packed snow-on-earth of the parade field as the rows of *paradematnyes* began stamping their feet in unison. An unearthly scream followed his own footsteps as he stepped off, lost and silent in the still-falling snow.

He shook his head, clearing it of the smoke and sound. His stomach growled. Not many people still attended these organized demonstrations in full anymore. Most simply showed their faces for the morning reconciliation. He would have to eat on the train.

The railhead was nestled deep within the dirigible yards. The narrow path traversed the canyons of steep wood and metal landing platforms. Hundreds of the structures reached up toward the sky, lost in the low-lying clouds that held back the snow for a moment. Between some of the platforms, the bellies of the dirigibles poked through the cloud cover, like a pregnant woman caught *en deshabille* after her bath.

Gas lamps lit the platforms, fading as the distance doubled. They stood, solemn custodians of the yards, reminding those seeking the station that the reach of the Empire extended much further than the tracks earlier dynasties had laid. Any person wishing to travel would thus be reminded of the extent of the bear's embrace, and the futility of trying to escape it.

Karl paused for a moment in the dark. He removed his hat, shaking the moisture from it against his leg. The glint of gaslight on steel caught his eye.

The *poyestkatnye* stood in heavy ranks in front of dirigible platforms, waiting for the operators to set the *bloodspark* that would jolt them to mechanical life. The lanky *matnyes* rested silently, joints gleaming with the lubricants necessary to keep them mobile as they operated the leviathans through the tropical environments of water and salt. The red Cyrillic lettering across their chests identified them as the tangible final products of his collective.

Karl had seen the flickering images of silver and light, projected by the operators who returned, wasted and malformed from their incredible explorations that sent the tendrils of glory and fame trickling back to the Empire on the shoulders of these strange creatures, twisted and scarred by their travels under inhospitable climes.

He passed a small cohort of operators, swarming down from their airship. They were swarthy, dressed in the silks of the East under their fur and leather. Most of the members of their ranks came from the subjugated countries of the Far East, their inhabitants accustomed by destiny and national predilection to travel beyond the confines of the Empire's dominion, and missed less sorely when they failed to return. As he passed, the three men swept their conical hats into a deep obeisance, then jumped back up as he continued by, unheeding. He heard the rattling of their keys and vials as they scurried off to continue the preparations for this new journey.

Karl had heard rumors of the Great Exploration. He had forgotten what number this was. There had been too many to count. Similar voyages had spent years mapping the North African tribal lands, questing deep into the continent in search of the hidden origin of the Nile.

He had little personal use for these journeys of strange fantastic sunlight and fields of lush, organic soil. Not for him rivers that ran muddy beneath the midday sky, even though rumors spread like oil on water about the great river on the new continent that promised a great green wealth of discovery.

His interest in these voyages stemmed rather more from business instincts than any romantic or patriotic feeling. He rarely admitted this fact in polite conversation and tended in fact to avoid most attempts at such. He no longer suffered the snide remarks concerning his bourgeois affiliations. His Teutonic legacy was evident in his name, but his Science had been sufficient to make his way through the upper echelons of, if not society, than at least those necessary for the greatness of the Empire.

He emerged from the forest of steel and stamped his way up the steps of the depot, shaking snow from his boots at each platform. The mighty ranks of the *poyestkatnye* and their faithful herder operators faded behind him. Karl had built a great collective from the ashes of Germany's subjugation. The Chief Machinist had been the key; his loss was unexplainable and, perhaps, irrecoverable. A vast, cold emptiness stretched before Karl, formed from the absent answers to the questions raised by the paper he still carried tucked into his aging satchel.

The whispers started when he reached the camp. They swirled up with gusts of snow that marked his path from the sleigh. The workhorses tossed their heads, the lubrications firing behind their eyes.

Karl stepped well away from them as he disembarked the sleigh. The bitter cold of the northlands sometimes played havoc on the gears, one of the reasons he traveled by rail and sleigh rather than trust the mighty air engines crafted in his own collective. The snow collected on his shoulders and in the tops of his boots as he trudged the short distance to the small wooden headquarters building.

Brigadier Lev, in a resplendent commandant's uniform that had seen better days, did not bother to get up from the table. He poured a glass of vodka and pushed it toward Karl.

"You know what the workers are saying?" he asked.

Karl took the vodka. "Enlighten me, Brigadier."

Lev whispered the name so softly, it was lost in a gust of wind that shook the flimsy structure. The small fire burning in the metal stove guttered, died, and was reborn as the wind left it.

"Old wives' tales," Karl said. "Told by the enslaved to put unease into the hearts of their conquerors."

He sniffed the vodka. With a shrug, he tossed the contents of the glass. The liquid was lost in the myriad of stains already adorning the wooden floor.

Karl set the glass back on the table. Lev stared at him, perhaps regretting the loss of the offering.

"Come with me, Brigadier," said Karl.

The wind shook the building once again, and Karl thought fleetingly that perhaps the cold was the cause for the commandant's pale cheek.

"Uh ... Comrade Engineer ... perhaps I could..."

"Brigadier, the newspaper informs me a man is dead in your camp," Karl said. "Not just any man. Kirlisoveyitch is dead. Your failure to resolve the cause of this matter is grounds for demotion at the least."

What the worst might be, he left unspoken. Lev asked no more questions, but grabbed the bottle from the table, plopped a fur cap over his bald head, and bowed low. "Permit me to accompany you, Comrade Engineer."

"Have a man see to the workhorses." Karl had not even bothered to remove his gloves. "I will need them for my return."

The two men left the lights and nominal warmth of the building behind them. Not far from the headquarters, they met a short, rather obese man hurrying toward the building. He waddled up, doffing his cap, bowing to the two. He caught a good look at Karl and bowed even deeper. Karl observed that the motion uprooted his shirt from his pants to expose his skin to the snow, which fell now in earnest.

"Dog." Lev kicked snow at the man. "See to the Comrade Engineer's workhorses."

Dog smiled and bowed again, then leaped to gather the steamworks under his care.

"He is not quite right in the senses," Lev said, following Karl's stare, mistaking impatience for concern. "But he has a gift with the machines."

"I do not wish to stand in the snow to discuss your men," Karl said. "Where is Kirlisoveyitch?"

"His body was taken on the last barge to Moscow," Lev said. "His paperwork was in order and he had family there."

Karl frowned.

"Don't worry, Comrade Engineer," Lev hastened to reassure him. "We have graphed everything, preserving it in the nitrate archives."

"Take me to his shop." Karl had been there before, but during the long twilight several summers ago. The night and the snow had claimed any last bit of familiarity he once had with this particular camp.

"This way," Brigadier Lev said.

Karl noticed the sideways glance Lev cast outside the camp as he turned to lead the way further into the maze of the collective. He followed the Brigadier's gaze, but all he noted were the shadows that moved with the snow in the spotlights of the perimeter fence.

The fence was only recently built. It was not a prison fence, and if one looked closely, one could discern that it had been set in a defensive posture rather than one to indicate confinement. In the past few years, wolves had discovered the grounds and had come out of the pines under the new moon to find those who stumbled, lost in the solace of sleep or drink.

The collective sent hunting parties after the wolves. They armed themselves with the latest longarms with the rifled barrels that sent the bullets flying farther and truer than ever before, fed by the breech-loading magazines that sent the rounds through the weapon with the mechanical surety of their larger cousins, the dirigible crew arms.

Then they had sent rescue parties after those hunting parties and found only blood and tracks in the snow. Some of those tracks had not seemed particularly wolf like, and now the felling crews would venture out only under cover of the sun with as many armed guards as could be spared from the few that roamed the camp.

The area beyond the fence had been cleared fifty meters out, where the fallen snow met a dense ring of pine trees. They stood, almost impenetrable, silent in the hush of the steady snowfall. The forest wall was broken only in one place, where the River Magna flowed out of the woods on its meandering way through the camp, carrying on her back the great black barges of coal and steel. The white-capped waters masked a green-dark muscular power that kept the steam turning the mill and the coals glowing in the great furnaces of the machine.

The main camp factory was built right over the river, and this was where Kirlisoveyitch had spent his days overseeing the powerful melding of metal and gears into the strange shapes that guided the great airships.

"As you can see, we have suffered no great loss of productivity, Comrade Engineer." Lev spoke as they made their way onto the great floor. The night shift bent their backs to the coals and metal, looking like a great poster of the Empire meant to show the gleaming march of progress in the sweat and mettle of its workers.

"I expect your productivity to be maintained," Karl replied mildly. "What I am lacking are answers as to why my Chief Machinist is no longer here to supervise production."

Lev gave his answer in the staccato shadow of the tic that jumped in his cheek. The whispers had infiltrated his awareness. He had been in the camps too long, and Karl knew that there was no place outside of them for such a man as this.

The Brigadier lowered his head and mumbled the word once again. His voice was lost in the great din of the shop.

Karl cut him off with an abrupt gesture. "I wish to see Kirlisoveyitch's shop."

The Brigadier led the way across the great shop floor. The whispers followed them. The workers scarcely ceased their labors, but Karl felt their eyes on his back and their speculation in the murmurs that moved under the sounds of distressed metal.

Upyr...

The word accompanied every mysterious happening that chanced to occur in the northern nightlands. It infected the camps, passed from one mind to another, germinating in the ever-fertile imaginations of the men who lived in the dark and the snow.

Kirli had dismissed such stories, as he dismissed any such thing that set his great factory in delay. Karl had hired him for his unique scientific perspective and brute disregard for peasant superstition and had been well satisfied. But the whispers persisted even under the glare of the coals that powered the great machines that signaled to the world the dawn of a new age—a new Empire, no longer held in thrall by superstition and things that left strange marks in the snow.

When the camp was first built, Karl had often frequented Kirlisoveyitch's shop. He had been younger then, a student of the philosophy that men worked more diligently when their masters were about. Such would give them encouragement and show them that they were loved. Karl had found in the Chief Machinist a rare, vast talent that spoke to the Scientist in terms of brotherly understanding, an understanding that could be mistaken for deeper affection.

Karl was older now and cared no more for such philosophies. He no longer had the inclination to spend his winters in the cold soot of the mills or the sweat streaked hells of the factories. As such, the disorder and chaos of the space caused him to miss his tread in the door.

"What is this?" Karl asked, astonished.

"This is the Comrade Chief Machinist's shop." Lev sweated, even in the cold.

Karl swore a deep German oath that passed outside of Lev's understanding. "Surely, this is not how he left his affairs."

Lev stared at him. Karl noticed the Brigadier still held the bottle of vodka in the pocket of his coat, clutching it as if waiting for an opportune moment to take a stealthy draught.

"No one has been in here since the body was taken away," Lev said.

"Since Kirlisoveyitch was taken away." Karl kept his voice tight, unemotional.

"Yes, Comrade Engineer." The understanding of the correction once again slid past the Brigadier's comprehension, and Karl was suddenly tired of his presence.

"Wait for me outside, Brigadier."

Lev nodded and stepped quickly outside, closing the door behind him. Karl felt the relief emanating from the man, both from the removal of his presence and for the opportunity to revisit the bottle.

Karl removed his leather gloves, tucking them deep into one of his pockets, and rubbed the bridge of his nose with two fingers, then passed the palm of his hand over his chin.

"Comrade Chief Machinist," Karl mused absently. "What was it you feared so greatly you did not even send word before cutting your own thread?"

No answer came in return, not even a whisper from the wind that piled snow around the wide glass windows. Karl looked up. The glass had to be quite thick to withstand the winter storms. It was held in place by many sturdy iron supports, steeply ramped to allow the snow to slide to the gutters. On a clear night it would be quite beautiful. Under the sun, it would be so bright as to be intolerable. Instinctively he shuttered his eyes and directed his gaze downward again.

A stale copper scent drew his attention. The brown stain, the splatter punctuated by scabby pulp, coated the papers piled deep on the long table.

The weapon lay to the side. It was a large pistol, the handle engraved with vines, pearl inlay set in around two Cyrillic characters. Karl picked it up, feeling the heft of the gun in his hand. He looked more closely at the engravings, recognizing the depiction. It was the Firebird, that great creation immortalized by the strings of the favored son of the

Empire. Karl wondered if there was some meaning behind that, or if the pistol was merely a convenient means to an end.

With one long fingernail, Karl scratched at the stain, curious. The long sheet of yellowing vellum appeared intact, and he could make out the long, red lines underneath the dried gore. The redprints emerged rather slowly from the scratching and he found a rag, soaked it in the steam bath, and wiped gently at the parchment. It was high quality. The blood streaked away, leaving the vellum and the printing intact.

Nothing. Or rather, a very mundane something. The sheaf of long parchments was merely a routine update of the intricate gears that *bloodsparked* the *paradematnyes*. While the street theatre *matnyes* were one of the main productions of this collective, Karl suspected that his Chief Machinist did not kill himself over what were essentially gigantic metal puppets.

"Brigadier Lev!" Karl raised his voice to be heard through the door.

There was a short delay and a fumbling with the doorknob. When Lev came back into the shop, the vodka bottle was not quite settled in his pocket.

Karl winced as the man gasped, grabbed, and missed at the bottle. It fell to the floor with a thump, but without the expected shatter. Lev turned red, scooped it back up, and settled it back into his jacket.

"Brigadier," Karl said. "Was Kirlisoveyitch working on anything else? Were any of his designs removed from his shop?"

"Oh no, Comrade Engineer," Lev said. "Everything is as we found it."

"Curious." Karl took his gloves from his pockets and began putting them back on. "The Chief Machinist I knew was always so..." He trailed off.

"We did allow men into the shop to remove the body," Lev said.

Karl turned on him, anger strengthening the lines of his face. "What did they touch?"

"Just the table where he was found." Lev cowered, his eyes wide, crouching before Karl's sudden ferocity. "And some of the equipment. They moved it only to remove the body."

"The body..." Karl's jaw tightened.

"Oh, don't worry," Lev said, once again misinterpreting the Comrade Engineer's reaction. "We have the archives—very thorough, yes. Before we even moved the remains to be prepared for their journey."

Karl straightened. The smell and taste of blood was in his senses, mingling with the faint odor of the burning gas from the lamps. It sickened him with its familiar miasma. He closed his eyes. He had seen much worse, but he did not want to see this.

———

The nitrate archives. The process was new and so prohibitively expensive as to limit its use to the very upper ranks of the Empire and, of course, the collective that was so recently home to the mind that birthed the technology.

Karl stood at the reader, selecting and moving lenses for optimum magnification. When he found the sharpness required, he straightened briefly, allowing his eyes to rest in the gloom from the reflected white light on the films.

Lev stared at him, less an active curiosity than a miniature trance brought on by boredom and sobriety. He spared a moment to wonder at the other man's perception of him. Tall, white hair, pale skin under his thick black furs and leather greatcoat. He had once selected his dress for the purpose of cutting an imposing figure. What was formerly intentional was now habit, and his manners and posture followed suit. He abruptly turned back to his lenses.

"These are all the archives set down in the room?"

"Yes, Comrade Engineer," Lev said.

"Who made the imprints?" Karl asked.

"Kirlisoveyitch's assistant." Lev's hand strayed to the pocket holding the bottle. "He taught him how to use the apparatus and imprint the archives on the nitrate."

"Kirli had an assistant?" Karl looked up sharply, raising one thin eyebrow.

"Someone to help in his shop, yes, Comrade Engineer." Lev's voice lifted, almost whining, and he shifted uneasily. "He was the one who found the body."

"Hm." Karl bent his head back to the lens. The archives showed him nothing unexpected. Whoever this assistant was, he knew both how to work the apparatus, as well as the necessary frames to archive the incident.

The archive of the workshop was clear and sharp, with no fuzzy or blurry images throughout the entire lens to suggest the presence of anything remotely uncanny. Karl had heard of extremely wealthy patrons who amused themselves by tricking the archives with "ghost images." He had been disinvited from these parties at which his collective's Science played the role of honored guest after he'd remarked that the "ghosts" looked like nothing more than simple flares that sometimes occurred when archiving in the bright sunshine. The only ghost in this image was the body that lay heavy in the frame, dwarfed by the imposing architecture of the shop.

Without lifting his gaze, Karl slipped the thick paper and silver archive out from beneath the lens and fixed a new one into the slot. A stark image of death greeted him. He had not realized until this moment, but he had been hoping for some small proof that this death, at least, had not been self-inflicted. That the last man Karl had counted on to remind him of his own humanity had not snuffed his own *bloodspark*. But the archive bore its silent, stubborn witness. He felt hope flicker and die out like the gas lamps in the winter ration periods.

"Comrade Engineer?" Lev's voice broke the silence Karl had not realized had settled around him. This deep in the bowels of the building, the wind was muted. The only sound in the room was of a faint humming. He realized it was the great engines of the mill, churning in their furnaces.

Karl lifted his head, gazing blankly past Lev. "Who was his assistant?"

"Dog," Lev replied.

"I wish to speak to him." Karl shifted his gaze to meet Lev's eyes.

Lev nodded. "Yes, Comrade Engineer, of course."

The Brigadier led him up the stairs, back onto the main factory floor. The smell of grease and other lubricants lay cold on the concrete. The Comrade Engineer's suspicions went whispering through the imposing structures of metal and ice, where men labored like ants on the giant leviathans that brought the conquering bear to her subjugated peoples. Below the whispers, the captive waters of the River Magna hurried the current along as workers unloaded the incoming barges and replaced their raw cargoes with the technology of the Empire.

Karl kept his distance from the running waters; his eyes observed the clockwork precision of the laborers, but his mind was consumed with the need to understand.

Brigadier Lev led the way back out of the great shop. Karl followed at a distance just long enough to discourage any attempts at conversation or explanation. There was very little Lev could say now, in any case. Once out of the heat of the shop, the cold reasserted itself. The snow continued to fall thickly, haloing the perimeter fence spotlights.

An unearthly howl stopped Lev in his tracks. Karl heard the faint click of one of the repeater longarms in the perimeter tower. Lev, Karl, the tower guards—all froze in tableaux to see what might emerge. A curious call, almost a questing sort of whine, carried through on the cold night air, muffled by the storm but still audible.

"Brigadier." Karl's voice jolted the man back to awareness. "Let us continue before I am frozen to the very ground."

"Yes, Comrade Engineer." Lev started walking again, a short fumbling stride. Karl noticed that he never took his eyes off the perimeter as they made their way past the pine woods.

Upyr...

Karl shook his head at the thought of it. It seemed every year the peasants dreamed up one more fairy tale goblin to populate the dark woods at the edge of the camp.

If this were twenty years ago, there might have been someone living outside the walls of the collective. They would have been spies or, more likely, saboteurs, although their numbers had dwindled. Many of them now resided in the same camps they had sought to overthrow. All had learned the futility of dancing with the bear.

Dog's billet was a small room off one of the main barracks buildings. Karl questioned the fat little man's solitary quarters, but Lev assured him that he had been steadfastly ejected from

every other billet. As adept an assistant as he was to
Kirlisoveyitch, no one else in the camp wished to remain in
his presence for an overabundance of time.

Upon stepping into the room, Karl understood why. The
man popped up from his chair, bowing obsequiously and
smiling in a vacuous manner guaranteed to creep the blood of
any normal man. The gas burning in the pair of wall sconces
barely illuminated the room; instead it merely added to the
sour smell of filth.

Lev hesitated in the threshold.

"Wait for me outside, Brigadier," Karl said. "Close the door
behind you."

Lev sighed in what might have been relief, his hands
closing on the bottle in his jacket even before the door was
shut firmly behind him.

Dog sat back down on his stool, his feet barely touching
the floor. He swung them back and forth like a child while he
waited expectantly, staring unashamed at Karl.

The Comrade Engineer ignored the assistant's presence
for a moment, allowing his eyes to adjust to the gloom in the
small apartment. It did not take long. He realized that what he
took at first for darkness were actually shadows that congealed
along walls piled from floor to ceiling with shelves and shelves
of clutter and junk.

Dog kept smiling, although his feet swung faster and faster
as Karl moved closer to the shelves, reaching out a hand to
sort through some of the junk. The collection had been there
for a very long time. Some of the debris was coated in dust
several inches thick, while other pieces gleamed lubricated
metal in the reflection from the gas lamps.

"This is your own private little workshop, isn't it?" Karl
asked the little goblin of a creature, who grinned and nodded
back. "You collect all manner of gears and clockwork, eh?"

Dog nodded again, or rather paused in his nodding and then started up again. He smiled wider and Karl realized that he nodded because with his stump of a tongue, he could no longer speak.

An odd feeling of distaste overwhelmed Karl. He wanted to leave the tiny, dirty room with the half-idiot grinning his child's grin, sitting, waiting. He swallowed the gorge that rose in his throat and coughed gently to clear it.

"You helped Chief Machinist Kirlisoveyitch in his shop, didn't you?" Karl spoke to Dog as he imagined one would speak to a child. Dog nodded and smiled. A gurgling sound came from his throat at the mention of his former master.

Something rustled in a corner of the room. It was too dark for vision to penetrate the gloom, but the sound caught Karl's attention.

"Did the Chief Machinist ever give you ... papers?" Karl used his hands with the long, thin fingers to describe what he was looking for. "They would be about the size of three books put together ... with images, lines, drawn on them in red?"

Dog nodded again and smiled. Karl closed his mouth around a snarled curse. He was severely discomfited. He rarely used profanity. The smell of the room thickened, if that were possible, the thick air almost a taste in his mouth.

"Where?" Karl asked. "Get them for me."

The tone of his command finally struck the smile from Dog's face. The little ogre hopped off his stool, his face a picture of reproach to the man who spoke to him thus.

Karl heard rustling, chattering, more of the peculiar guttural chortling. The room did not seem so large as to allow the man to disappear from his sight, but it was a long moment before Dog reappeared from the shadows clutching several scrolls and sheaves of vellum.

Karl went to take them, but Dog stopped short just out of reach.

"Give those to me." Karl held out a gloved hand.

Dog shook his head, obstinate.

"Chief Machinist Kirlisoveyitch was my friend," Karl said. "If he gave those to you, he meant for you to keep them safe for me."

Dog looked at him doubtfully, then down at the pages he held clenched in his stubby fingers. Karl noted with distaste that several of the prints were permanently creased from his crushing grip. Finally, Dog extended his arm to Karl, who took the prints. Dog shuffled backwards from his reach, a curious light burning in his eyes as he watched the Comrade Engineer leave the room. As the door closed, the light burned brighter, as if someone had turned a flame under some gas lamp, before burning completely out.

Karl waited until he was back inside the flimsy headquarters building before removing his gloves and unrolling the printed pages with their promised designs. He could tell Brigadier Lev was burning with a most unseemly curiosity, but banished the commandant to his small room. Lev's presence in the company of Kirlisoveyitch's last masterpiece was unwelcome.

The final unrolling of the parchment on the unsteady table was anticlimactic. There were no grand flourishes to accompany the reveal. Even the wind that had so buffeted the structure earlier in the night seemed to have died quietly.

In his small room, nursing the last of his pathetic bottle, Brigadier Lev paused. He held his breath without realizing it. The sound coming from the outer room was a mixture of triumph and grief, expressions he had not thought the great Comrade Engineer capable of making.

Alone, Comrade Engineer Karl von Tauben gazed at his late friend's greatest success. A shudder went through him as he traced the fallen red lines with one manicured finger. Here was the great Weapon he had sought, the most powerful ever designed. This would be the legacy of his collective. This would be the legacy of the great *Atomatnyes*. And the Empire would forever equate the victory of the bear with the vindication of his camps.

Karl delved into the ever more intricate designs. He read in them a great, terrible destruction, this final *matnye* a weapon too great to be used, too terrible not to be built. A strange excitement kindled in him, paled his cheek in the overwhelming ferment that agitated his desire.

An indescribable sound echoed through the camp, muffled below the soft wind and the snow that continued to fall silently. The men on the shop floor momentarily paused feeding the great giant beasts their diet of coal. In his tiny apartment, Dog hesitated before adding his own weird chortle to the sound, hooting along as it rose and fell. Across the perimeter, the tower guards lifted and primed their long barrels, tense in the dark. In his own small room, Brigadier Lev fingered the small caliber pistol tucked into the drawer of the table next to his desk. The commandant crossed himself in an unconscious gesture he had learned and forgotten many years before.

Karl threw the pages to the ground in a gesture of casual hatred. He swallowed back his agitation, the excitement that still crawled along his limbs. The *Atomatnyes* would never be built, not in the anticipated future of the von Tauben collective. The designs captured in the painstakingly formed red lines were too advanced for even the great craftsmen that toiled on the floors of the Comrade Engineer. The machines to build these new beasts would have to be designed themselves.

The success was incomplete, and so the Chief Machinist had met with failure. The minute progress grasped and eked by the Comrade Engineer and his workers would be set back so many years, it would be a wonder if they received any of the great Commissions from the Empire for another hundred years. Karl steadied himself on the table with both hands. If he were extremely unlucky, the collective and all of its great machines would pass into the hands of another. He bared his teeth and hissed.

The whispers—did the entire camp know of what Kirlisoveyitch had discovered? Did they thus understand the choice he had made? Karl had come to the camp with his unspoken hope and been met with the cold red iron of certainty.

Kirli had been a suicide. That much was certain. Hiring Kirli had been the closest Karl had ever come to having a brother. He had killed himself knowing the failure would certainly bring Karl to the camp. And though Karl surely loved the Chief Machinist as well as he could, there would have been no way to spare him the consequences of that failure. His last act of design had been to free Karl of the onerous duty of killing his friend.

"Herr Comrade Engineer?" Brigadier Lev stood at the door, uncertain.

Karl turned slowly to face him, and Lev saw his face, ravaged with the attempt to express the grief that lay cold on the snow. As the Brigadier stared, the skin around the Engineer's eyes lifted and twisted. The corners of his mouth turned, and he smiled. The grimace offered promises of blood and iron, and in that one glimpse Lev understood that the shadows to fear lay not beyond the ring of pines fifty meters outside of camp, but had been brought to the collective in the person of its overlord.

Karl mounted the sleigh. The workhorses were primed and eager to be off, clanking their gears and steamsnorting in anticipation. There was no sign of Dog, but Karl did not worry. The little man would either die of cold and exposure, or return to the forest from where he had surely come. The shadows watching the camp would soon make their cold way in to reclaim the clearing from which they had only temporarily been banished.

The buildings behind him lay stiff and silent. The great engines of the camp shop still churned: the current of the river and embers of the coal would power them until they fell to disrepair and ruin. The sympathetic flames leaped from the roof of the shop, gathering the barracks, the headquarters building, the stables and the carefully built towers of the perimeter fence into the fire's embrace.

This was Comrade Engineer Karl von Tauben's last, great gift to the man who had come closest to the appellation of friend. The cold body of the Chief Machinist made its way somewhere in the night along the waters of the River Magna, but his cenotaph would be writ here—not as a cold, granite monument, but in the death and fire of the great collective. Chief Machinist Kirlisoveyitch's last designs curled and crumpled in the flames, an offering on the pyre to the gods of the age of steam and steel.

The Comrade Engineer lit the *spark* in the workhorses. The dawn was close, although the blizzard tamped out any light under its lashings of rain-driven snow. The workhorses stamped their feet as they started off through the cold, which failed to reach the blood of the man in the sleigh. The satisfaction of his hunger burned him from the inside, illuminating the frustrated anger and despair that followed him from the camp. In the tracks of the sleigh, the blood ran deep black against the moonlit snow, taking its true red form only where the firelight kissed it briefly before dying into embers.

SLITHER

THE GAME DIDN'T SEEM THAT HARD. IN THE WINDOW THAT popped up on the glowing screen, it was a five-by-five square box with one black circle and one white circle positioned next to each other at the top center of the box.

The instructions materialized in another pop up.

Welcome to Slither, the game where you slide your way to victory! Find your way around your opponent to the other side of the board. First one there, wins!

That was it.

Mel was in the middle of a language lesson and had run out of extra points, so she had clicked on the option to watch an ad and gain more hearts. This game, Slither, had popped up. Usually Mel let the required time elapse and then just clicked it closed to go back to her Gaelic lesson, but this time, she let her finger hover over the screen.

The touchpad on this new phone was super sensitive. Without even touching the glass, the game had popped up with its easy instructions.

Curious, Mel grabbed the black icon with her thumb and

tried to move it. She couldn't get it to go straight forward; when she tried that and released the ball, the little icon slipped back to its starting position. Next, she tried moving diagonally. This time, she had no problem depositing the little black ball in front of the white one.

Having played more than her fair share of mindless phone games, Mel expected to see the white ball go around, heralding a game of leapfrog to the end of the square.

Not much of a challenge. Whoever starts first wins.

She looked for the "x" that would close the ad and take her back to her language app, but it had disappeared. Even touching the tip of her finger to the screen didn't bring it up. Instead, on the screen, the white ball jumped over the black one.

The moment the white ball landed on the other side, the entire screen turned a bright red, even the edges outside the game's window.

"Ah, fuck." Mel frantically tried to close the window, cursing again as the red screen persisted. "What the hell is this?"

The red faded and cleared, and the screen was back. This time, the game had multiplied and there were ten squares across each side. Two black balls and two white balls nestled at the top this time. A message popped up.

Welcome to Slither, the game where you slide your way to victory! Find your way around your opponent to the other side of the board. Don't be the last one there!

"Don't be the last one there?" Mel read aloud. "Forget this."

She pressed the buttons that hard started the phone, hoping that turning it off and bringing it back up afterwards would fix whatever issue the game had caused on her phone.

She was definitely going to have to submit something to the language app, letting them know that one of their advertisements was some kind of malware.

"Ah, *fuck.*" This time, she muttered the words, pitching her voice low so her neighbors wouldn't hear and complain again about profanity in the workplace.

The lockscreen appeared just fine, and she used her thumb to open it up. The first screen of apps appeared as normal, free and clear, but after a few seconds, the familiar grid pattern of the game faded in and took over the screen.

"Crap. I'm gonna lose my streak."

Mel turned the phone all the way off and tossed it on her desk. She was going to have to get it looked at, and anyway, her lunch break was over. Powering up her work computer, she opened the spreadsheet she had been working on after that morning's meeting.

The familiar grid lines and cross-sections popped up, color coded and organized, a complete map of her department's expenditures by the month. It would be a matter of an hour or so to match the expenditures to the receipts, review for anything weird or over the approved limit, sign it, and send it forward. Then, maybe she could grab an afternoon coffee and see about calling someone about the phone.

Her cursor froze on the screen. She moved the mouse around, then attempted to use the mouse pad to unfreeze the little arrow.

"C'mon, dammit." She glared at the screen. *What is it with technology—always at the worst time.* Maybe it was time to get that afternoon coffee.

A familiar square started forming on the screen, pale at first, then gradually becoming less and less translucent, until it took up almost the entire screen. This time, the squares had grown yet again, to a twenty-by-twenty box, with three black and three white balls at the top, arranged in an alternating pattern.

Welcome to Slither!

Mel stood up, looking over the three-quarter gray fabric walls that portioned off her little cubicle from the others on the floor. *Is someone fucking with me?* She couldn't think of who it might be. Nor, looking around, did she see anyone popping their head up, casting an eye around the cube farm to see who might be reacting to their dumb prank.

Sitting back down, she hovered her fingers over the alt-ctrl-delete button sequence. She'd lose some work shutting down like that, but it was better that than yet another lecture from the geeks in the IT department. Mel wasn't even sure how playing a game on her phone had infected her computer, but she didn't want to hear about it.

Without warning, a high-pitched *BEEEEEE—* erupted from the computer speakers.

Mel panicked, and tried to turn it off, turn the monitor off, turn the volume down, unplug the computer— The sound went on, each fraction of a second seeming like a year. Finally, she lunged for the mouse, clicked on one of the black balls and dragged it one diagonal space.

Like magic, the sound shut off.

"What the heck was that, Mel?" A head popped over the cube wall. Stan, her cube mate on the other side. "You get some feedback?"

She smiled, still feeling the heat in her cheeks and the shake of the post-adrenaline rush. "Yeah. Something. Feedback. Ugh. Technology."

Stan chuckled. "It's the worst." Shaking his head, he disappeared from view.

On the screen, Mel looked where she had moved the ball. She had grabbed it and shifted it to the side, advancing, yet out of the path of the white ball. On screen, one of the center white balls pulsed, then moved, settling directly in front of one of her black balls. Mel, remembering the first game, clicked on the black ball and leapfrogged it over the white one. With a sickening crunch, the white one dissolved and faded.

Mel breathed deeply. She didn't know what was going on, but if all she had to do was play a game to get her computer back, she could do that. Carefully, she moved another ball, staying out of the line of attack of the white balls.

Slowly, the white and black balls advanced down the screen, Mel mostly in the lead. As her first ball reached the end of the square, she moved it into the line, expecting— hoping—to see it release her from the screen. Instead, another white ball moved into a new position.

"Crap." Mel closed her eyes. *Okay, no problem, the rest of the balls are almost there. Christ.*

Without thinking, she moved her black ball into the path of the white one. This time, the white one wasted no time in jumping her piece. The screen flashed red, but Mel barely noticed.

Instead, her attention was focused on the screaming pain from the shallow furrow along her right forearm. *Whatthehell, whatthehell, whatthehell?*

The red faded away, leaving the game as before. Mel stared at her arm until a soft warning *beep* sounded. Once. Twice, a little louder. Three ti—

She cut it off, clicking her last black ball and sliding it into place at the end of the block.

Congratulations, Slither Resident! You have leveled up!

From across the cube farm, a scream started, an anguished cry of pain that went on and on until Mel and Stan and everyone else on the floor had popped up, searching for the source, heads rotating left and right like so many corporate gophers.

"Do you see Luz?" Stan asked.

Mel shook her head. The scream abruptly cut off. Luz was in accounts receivable, a short, spry woman with a twinkle in her eye and a fondness for bringing delicious home-baked Mexican pastries to share with the office on Fridays.

Oh, God. Had she been playing against Luz? On the game? Jesus Christ, what the hell was happening?

Mel bent to her computer, hitting alt-ctrl-delete as fast as she could. The screen went dark as the computer powered down.

So did the lights.

The rest of the office was still standing, still wondering what was going on. They hadn't started milling around again, just hanging out in their little cubes, looking at each other. One or two cracked a joke about paying the electric bill.

The darkness grew, cutting off even the small amount of light that came from computer screens and phone flashlights.

No. Oh, God. No.

The light went completely out, the darkness total.

A white light appeared overhead, the illumination slowly spreading until it had evenly lit the entire area where Mel stood with her colleagues. The gray fabric cube walls were gone, replaced by two-inch-wide, even lines that demarcated where their cubes had been.

It looked exactly like—*but how can it be?*

Mel tightened her grasp around the knife in her right hand.

The words formed above them, coalescing from nothing into a familiar, opaque script.

Welcome to Slither, the game where you slide your way to victory!

As always, Mel made the first move.

READERS

DWIGHT HATED WALKING INTO THE LIVING ROOM AND FACING HIS wife's completely non-virtual collection of books, displayed unfashionably in the first space in the house their guests would see. Even as newlyweds, he had barely tolerated her need for the physical nature of the books, and after a few years quit making excuses to guests for the queer habit and instead insisted that all visitors come around to the side of the house.

If she read any of the books more than once, he would have been less agitated when he thought about it. More often than not, though, he would walk into the room and find her sitting in a chair nodding over her own reader, immersed in yet another new virtual purchase. Dwight had once, just as an experiment, taken one book from a bottom shelf and hidden it, to see if she would notice. She had not spoken a word, but two days later, he found his closet in disarray and the book back on the bottom shelf of the collection.

Rhonda caught him in there late the night of their tenth wedding anniversary, tipping back the dregs of the latest social gathering.

"How much do you think these are worth?" he asked, running his finger along the length of spines. Some were well worn and broken, others virginally smooth underneath the soft pads of his fingertips.

Rhonda shrugged and held the door to the hallway open, hinting that it was time for him to put down his drink and head down the hall to bed.

"I don't know," she said. "Most of them were mass-market publications."

"Not everybody collects these things," Dwight said. "Where do you think they've all gone?"

His attention had been piqued by an offhand comment from one of their guests, a man of some standing from Dwight's office whom they invited mostly because it was the smart thing to do. But the man's attention was enough to set the wheels of potential avarice turning.

"What about this one?"

Rhonda winced to see the alcohol in her husband's glass slosh dangerously close to the volume he wrenched from the shelf. His hand closed around the book, causing him to angle his wrist awkwardly as he held it up for her to see.

"It used to be quite valuable," Rhonda said, weighing honesty against the chances of Dwight remembering anything about the evening through the next morning's hangover. "But nobody buys books these days, so the prices have fallen quite a bit."

He stared at her, uncomprehending. She stepped two paces toward him, and he held up his hands in surrender. The gesture caused the liquid in his glass to slop on his sleeve. He tried to fit the book back on the shelf, but his lack of coordination defeated his one-armed attempts to replace it, and he settled for sliding the book horizontally into place to lie on the shelf atop its siblings.

Later that night, Dwight safely sleeping in the bedroom after the obligatory, half-hearted attempt to physically celebrate their nuptials had passed, Rhonda sat at the table and re-read the notice on her reader. Their state allowance had been halved yet again, consequences of the economy and her recent fall from grace. Or, at least, her plummeting position in the Elementary Instructor Ratings.

She sighed. When she assigned the "Book" report, she knew not many people understood her obsession. At least for old, real books made of paper. Most everyone, but especially her young students, understood the concept of "books" to mean the digital works that appeared on their screens when they downloaded a purchase. "Books" had never gone away, simply transformed venues. Her attraction to the "real" thing was as confusing and abstract as would be a strange desire for old vacuum tubes and dial-up modems outside of the Museum of Technology and Innovation. She took her students there. Or used to, until the low ratings struck it from the curriculum.

"Well if there's one thing that hasn't changed, it's faculty meetings will never start on time." Jane's mouth was full from something she was snacking on, but the sarcasm came through loud and clear.

Rhonda turned as her fellow instructor slid into the seat next to her. The two sat in a long row of women in front of an array of video screens. Since the consolidation of the old school districts into federal zones, faculty meetings were held in huge teleconferencing systems. It was less a meeting than an experience in fighting boredom while some administrator carried on a one-way conversation with a faceless league of uninterested instructors. The Zone 3 Administrator, Michael Greene, could indeed be counted on to be at least ten minutes late, which meant that fully half of the screens were still blue to indicate the viewers had not yet logged on. Rhonda had been waiting for almost half an hour, screen live, wondering why she herself couldn't stop showing up ten minutes early for everything.

"Heard you got downrated," Jane said. "That's some wet toast."

Rhonda shrugged. It was a familiar gesture. Her ratings never started the school semester very high to begin with, and had steadily declined ever since she had started instructing five years ago. There had been the incident with the baseball player, whose grade she had changed from failing to a passing "C," not realizing that his parents and community wanted and expected an "A." She had fixed it of course, but her initial naiveté set up her reputation as the teacher who was not only boring, but didn't understand grades and how they related to the real world.

The Administrator's blue screen finally darkened and resolved to his image. Rhonda and Jane put their headsets on and turned up the volume. Rhonda tried to pay attention, but found her thoughts drifting as the Admin called roll and began rehashing the minutes of the last faculty meeting. That one had taken nearly four hours, and she was pretty sure that she was not going to miss anything by not paying attention.

They were going to have to move, Rhonda thought. With the diminished salary, they would not be able to afford the place they were staying. If there were some way they could justify the dwelling for a federal subsidy, they might have a chance, but federal opinion was that three bedrooms and two rooms was too much space for two people in the first place.

Downsizing would be expected. Unless, of course, she and Dwight upsized their family.

Rhonda had left her reader on the kitchen island. She came home to find Dwight frowning at it. He looked up at her expectantly as she walked in. She placed her small bag on the counter beside the device. Its green light blinked with the scores of student essays her charges were sending to her, essays that she would spend most of the night reading, grading, then re-grading to fit the scores with her students' parents' expectations.

"This could be a good thing," Dwight said. She looked at the screen, viewing her downgrade notice with detachment.

"Did you make anything for dinner?" she asked, noting the lack of dishes in the sink.

"I knew you had the faculty meeting, so I went out after work."

Rhonda sighed inwardly and resigned herself to scrounging a random snack later. There was some fruit in the refrigerator, she thought. Maybe a sandwich. Dwight set the reader down on the surface and gently placed his hands on her shoulders.

"This could be a sign, honey," Dwight said.

Rhonda steeled herself. "It's not a sign, Dwight."

She tried to keep the irritation out of her voice. It was going to be a long night of essay grading, and a fight wouldn't make it any more pleasant.

"But this would be the perfect time," Dwight said.

"I'm not a mother," Rhonda said. She refrained from mentioning that they had discussed this subject many times, including before they got married. They had, in fact, had many long discussions about their expectations regarding finances, children, religion, all the things couples were supposed to talk about before they got married. She had thought she was clear, but shortly after the ceremony realized that the two of them had been simply talking. What they had not been doing was understanding the other's side of the conversation. As a result, they continued their discussions past their wedding, past the eager infatuation of the first year or so, and on into the slog of eternal couplehood. Their discussions had gotten more heated, and then less heated. Finally, they settled into a series of short phrases, well-rehearsed codes of argument, until new material arose as grist for the conversation.

"I have plenty of friends who thought they didn't want kids until they had them," Dwight said. Rhonda thought of his friends, and how she felt a little sorry for Dwight as he watched his colleagues embark into fatherhood.

"I'm tired," Rhonda said. "That meeting went on forever."

The day's lesson was safe territory, at least for the time being. The students—half in attendance, half staring mutely through the videoscreen mosaic above her desk—had some modicum of interest in the history of organized sports in the federal states, and Rhonda thought that maybe her week's ratings wouldn't slide as grievously as normal.

As she taught, the instant feedback bar scrolled across the screen on her desk. There was a satisfying amount of green in the "Interesting Choice of Material" and "This Lesson Held My Attention" Likert scales. The columns measuring instructor engagement and interpersonal computer-mediated communication remained depressingly red.

Looking up at the screens, she attempted to catch the eye of one of the students. Any student. She flitted her gaze across the screens, lingering long enough to catch the eye if possible, but not so long that the student would be uncomfortable, exactly as she had learned in her first tele-education class. Their eyes remained glued to the graphics she was pumping through the feed—and the digital distractions endemic to their desktops. Even the students sitting in front of her managed to immerse themselves in their material, avoiding her eyes. She sighed and sent a mass text with the homework—a short essay on the historical sports team of their choice. The muffled groans reminded her that the students preferred multiple choice. The feedback bars across her desk turned uniformly red as the students trudged out of the room, the line of videoscreens above them fading to black.

"Want to grab a coffee?" Jane poked her head in the room.

Rhonda switched her screen off. She felt vaguely guilty about the red bars. She didn't want Jane to see them, wasn't up to dealing with the expressions of sympathy and mutual commiseration at the state of student appreciation and federal education these days.

"Can't," Rhonda said. "Lesson plans."

Jane grimaced. "They're a pain. Want some help?"

"No," Rhonda said, and then, because she worried Jane might think her abrupt: "Thank you."

Another teacher called to Jane, who leaned back from the door to answer the greeting. She looked in the room, then back at Rhonda. "Well, good luck with those lesson plans."

"Thank you," Rhonda said. "Good night."

Rhonda waited until Jane had left, listening to her footsteps as she hurried back down the corridor to catch up with her friend. She quietly collected her things, checking her reader for any messages from Dwight before stuffing it into her bag.

"Ten years." She said the words aloud, rolling them around in her mouth. They slipped from her and faded quickly in the flat, bright light of the empty room.

———

Dwight thought ten years was long enough to wait, and told her so over dinner. Their menu had become as routine as all the other important parts of their life. He left his peas on the side of the plate as he did every Friday night, placing his fork and knife over them. Rhonda used her utensils to scrape up the last of the vegetables from her own plate.

"It's time to make a decision," he said. He rested his elbows on the table, twisting the stem of his wineglass between his thumb and middle finger.

"I'm not having this conversation again," Rhonda said. "We agreed. Two salaries, no kids. That's the sort of life we said we wanted."

"Things change," Dwight said. "Ten years, and you're barely making the same salary as the first-year instructors. Heck, your friend Jane—she's what, been teaching eight years? She makes twice what you do."

Rhonda arched an eyebrow. She hadn't been aware Dwight discussed her salary with anyone.

"There's only one way we are going to keep this house without that salary," Dwight said.

"We don't have the room." Rhonda rested her forehead in her hand.

"We do have the room," Dwight said. His voice was even and well-modulated. "It's full of your useless crap."

In the quiet that followed, Rhonda gathered their plates

and took them to the kitchen. The clinking of the china in the sink set her nerves on edge. She listened to the sounds in the other room as Dwight pushed his chair away and headed to bed.

The library wasn't such a large room. The shelves took up about a third of the space that would be available if they were removed. A real estate agent had pointed that out at a party, throwing around words like "functional space" and "resale opportunity." Rhonda wondered what those words even meant.

She stood, silent, at the shelves, running her finger along the length of the spines, some well worn and broken, others smooth underneath the soft pads of her fingertips—her stack of books not yet read.

Here was an anthology of American short stories, smelling of glue and paper in an old blue cloth binding. Her grandfather had kept it at random from a college literature course. Its neighbor—tattered in green cloth and cardboard and falling apart—an autographed copy of a biography of Abraham Lincoln by Ida Tarbell. Two shelves below, a paperback copy of Stephen Hawking's book, which she kept meaning to read.

She inhaled. The scent took her back to her grandparent's basement down at the shore, shelves not dissimilar from these lining the wall, a dehumidifier bucket crankily catching the moisture that the machine sucked from the air. Even so, some of the books still showed a few scars where she had cleaned the mold from their covers. Most of these books had come from that inheritance, and Rhonda shivered a familiar frisson of pleasure as she thought of the worlds contained in their neat, even gray lines.

She pulled a book from the shelf, a well-worn copy of Ray Bradbury's *Fahrenheit 451*. It fell open to a passage, the spine broken in to where she had taken an extended pause in her reading, years ago. The pause had left its permanent imprint in the pages. Rhonda glanced impatiently over the words, letting them slide off her concentration. She closed the book and put it back on the shelf.

"Ten years."

Dwight woke to the most embarrassing thing his wife had ever done. The Saturday morning sun shone brightly down on the impeccably landscaped green of the housing district as he stumbled downstairs in his pre-caffeinated haze. Movement outside the window stopped him, and he looked twice to make sure he saw what he thought he was seeing.

Rhonda used her hip to nudge open the front door. Her hands were busy holding a cardboard box stacked high with books.

"What are you doing?" Dwight didn't realize he was shouting until his wife jumped and almost dropped the box. She tightened her grip on the load, pushed the door open, and went outside. Belatedly, Dwight realized she was taking books out of the house, not, as he feared, bringing in more to be added to the already monstrous collection.

He sighed in relief, until he realized she had set up a folding card table at the end of the driveway. He opened the door and stomped out to the end, trying to appear as if he and his wife disagreed often on Saturday mornings in their pajamas. In their driveway.

"What are you doing?" Dwight kept his voice down. "The HOA was pretty darn clear about yard sales."

"I'm not holding a yard sale, Dwight." Rhonda's tone was dismissive, as if Dwight was no more than one of her students, and not a very bright one at that.

Dwight stood there as his wife returned to the house. She had been at work for a while—boxes were packed and stacked around the card table. A hand-lettered sign hung off the edge of one of the boxes. It read: "Free to good home."

Rhonda deposited another box next to the overflowing stack.

"What are you doing?" Dwight asked again. "Nobody is going to want any of this stuff."

"You wanted the room," Rhonda said. "You've got the room. You can give me one more day."

She unfolded a camp chair and set it up beside the table. Propping her still-shapely legs on one of the boxes, she selected a novel and began to read.

"These are all going to still be here until the end of the day," Dwight said. "You should just let me take them to the recycling center."

"Go back in the house, Dwight," Rhonda said. "I made you coffee."

Dwight was correct. At the end of the day, all the books were still at the end of the driveway. Rhonda waited until the sun had set before standing up, stretching to work out the kinks. She had caught a bit of sun on her face and neck, and slapped a mosquito. It was getting cooler.

It was still light enough out to read. She picked up a book one last time, read a few sentences, then closed it and put it back on the pile.

Dwight watched from the kitchen window. She smiled a

crooked, halfway grin, to see him frowning so hard. She wondered if the lines etched on his forehead were from worry about her, or about what the neighbors were thinking. She smiled wider.

The books were dry, and the day had been hot. Rhonda didn't bother with any sort of starter. She pulled a book of matches from her pocket, a small packet like the ones they used to sell in bars, or give you at the supermarket when you bought a pack of cigarettes and a couple of magazines.

She lit the first match and tossed it onto the pile. It burned steadily, then caught a paperback cover, accentuating the colors on the lurid frontispiece as it flared and crinkled them into black ash.

Rhonda struck another match. This one she placed carefully on the right side of the stack. The little flames started to creep toward each other across the vast paper landscape.

The third match sputtered and died, blowing away in the little evening breeze that sprung up. She sheltered the fourth match, and it lit easily. She shielded it with her body as the conflagration took, held and began to dance in earnest.

"Rhonda!" Dwight's voice was drowned by the flames. They reached high enough in the air to provide a welcome spectacle to the entire neighborhood. He danced around the blaze with his home fire extinguisher, trying to remember where he was supposed to aim the stream, which seemed completely useless in quenching the fire. "Rhonda!"

Sirens announced the arrival of the firefighters. They pushed him professionally away from the burning collection, and into the arms of the federal police who wanted to know what he thought he was doing, setting a blaze like this in a residential area and if there was some underlying political message behind the event. And, what in the world was he doing with all of those books?

Dwight looked for his wife, but she was nowhere to be found.

MEMBRANE

THE EMPTY HOSPITAL WAS A HORROR MOVIE CLICHÉ, BUT THE sirens had sounded sixteen hours ago, and now the corridors resembled the paper-and-medical-debris-strewn halls of Hollywood's finest set design.

The evacuation plan sat in its pristine binder in the Director's office. The pages, crisp and unwrinkled, hadn't been disturbed since they slid smoothly off the printer, three-hole punched by a clerk, stuck in the binder with its distinctive "Cypress Heights General" stamped on the cover, and deposited to the shelf after the annual tabletop exercise.

From their vantage point under the Director's large, solid-wood desk, Sam could see the white spine of the binder, lined up in a row with other spotless binders full of protocol and standard operating procedures.

Nothing in there had even been remotely useful. Nobody had even tried to open them.

Sam was—had been—three weeks into a student nursing internship at Cypress Heights, barely long enough to learn where the good bathrooms were, and which residents to avoid.

They hadn't been there last year when the hospital staff

had earned high marks in the chosen scenario—a pre-evacuation in the face of peaceful protests turned into violent riots and looting. It didn't matter that the staff had written its own test scenario, one that included an overwhelmed ER and blocked streets with emergency vehicles unable to navigate. The hospital doctors and nurses and internists and actors dressed in moulage all performed at the highest of levels, and the Director got a plaque and a binder of *lessons learned* that sat, collecting dust, on the shelf.

The desk was a good place to hide. A good place to stay. Sam swallowed back a cough and wiped their cheek with the back of their hand, the stubble on their jaw rough against their skin. They'd been under the desk longer than they thought. Long enough for the lights to flicker and fade, and the daylight to take their place. Long enough for the alarms to run out of battery and die, for the screams and the feet pounding in the corridors to fade into dead silence.

Sam had been assigned to the respiratory ward, with a resident who kept referring to them as "dude," and who was supposed to show them the finer parts of working with a patient currently undergoing extracorporeal membrane oxygenation. They didn't expect to ever work with ECMO patients; as the resident explained, it required a specially trained nurse to administer the anticoagulants and monitor for infections and correct sedation levels. But again, they were new, and the senior nurse did not have much time or patience for explaining things, so Sam had been told to observe, which they interpreted as: "Stay quiet and out of trouble until we find a good place for you."

The first wave of evacuation had been everyone who could walk or run or hurry, led by a group of nurses who shepherded them through the halls and down the stairs. There were supposed to be more groups after that, orderly rows of triaged patients, but after the first wave, when the panic hit and people started shoving and pushing, everything had gotten muddled.

Sam had been left in the chaos, handed a chart and forgotten, sweating under their layers of mask and gloves and face shield and sterile clothing cover. That resident had stared at them, told them: "Keep an eye on the patient," and left them there when the sirens went off and the announcements started blaring through the loudspeakers. The words had been completely indistinguishable, an unscripted emergency that no one could comprehend until the chaos was too complete.

In the hours that passed in the silence, Sam had waited. The waiting grew harder and harder. They'd stepped away from the patient only for a moment, to find a bathroom, in hallways that for once were not full of people watching to see which door they chose to use. The entire floor was quiet and empty, even when they came out.

Sam had tried the phone at the nurse's station, but there was nothing on the other end when she picked it up, not even a busy signal. Their phone was in their locker on the ground floor, and they had decided to go down quickly and come back up. No one was around to notice, and their patient was comatose.

They'd shuffled down a few floors, then stopped to look through the fireproof glass at one of the landings. Out in the hall of the oncology department, they'd finally spotted people. Or rather, bodies. Sprawled. In pieces. Painting the hall in macabre shadows.

There, in the middle of the hall, a figure. Short, thin, almost child-like, it stooped over a wheelchair, like a concerned child. At least that's what Sam thought, until the figure straightened, and they saw the red smears, the matted hair, the way the arms of its victim flopped over the sides of the chair.

Sam had almost screamed. Instead, they pounded back up the stairs in their plain, white Asics and sprinted to their patient. They'd stood beside his bed in indecision, unsure, then had finally switched everything over to battery power, unhooking the various wires and tubes and rearranging them to prep the patient for transport.

They'd pushed the patient out of the room with its wide glass windows, meant for easy observation, the small ECMO device tucked into his side, beeping as it pumped blood from one side of the membrane to the other.

On this floor, the only room without those large windows was the Director's office. It had a door with a small window, but she had papered it over. Sam had headed for it, pushing the patient bed in front of them, only to come up short against the doorjamb. There was no way they were going to fit the bed with its patient through the narrow entrance.

The silence had been deafening as Sam had stared at the conundrum. With the blood rushing in their ears, it seemed as if the empty halls echoed and clamored. It was only when an actual sound broke the silence that Sam realized how still it had become.

The sound was a thump somewhere, and Sam hadn't stopped to see where it was coming from. They had abandoned their patient there in the hallway and, with a sob, thrown themselves into the room, closing the door and locking it behind them, then hunkering under the desk until their limbs cramped and numbed.

"Hello?" It came out as a croak, as Sam whispered around the saliva that had dried in their throat. They coughed and tried again. "Hello?"

They hadn't been wrong. They *had* heard something, out

in the hallway. Was it their patient? No. Their patient was... They had abandoned their patient, left him out there with that ... *thing.*

Sam began to cry, deep, gulping, silent sobs. Shaking, they crawled forward, pulling themselves up, supporting themselves as they hunched over their desk, gritting their teeth against the pins and needles as blood flow returned to their lower limbs.

The thump came again. Not a knock, more like something stumbling against the door as it moved past.

Sam was a student nurse, on an internship. That wasn't their patient out there. It was *a* patient. Probably a dead patient. Even the little ECMO couldn't keep them going. The battery had to have run out. The anticoagulant failed. Something. He couldn't be alive. They muttered that under their breath as they shuffled to the door, putting their ear to the heavy wood. Nothing. Wishing they had more fingernails, they pried at the paper covering the small window. They were still wearing their face shield, which now sat cockeyed on their head.

Finally, the paper, which was more like a thick sticker over the window, peeled away. Instead of giving them a view of the hallway, there was a film of red splatter that obscured their vision.

Was that another thump?

No. Just Sam once again hearing things in the silence.

They'd only seen one of those things. And it was small. Sam wasn't that tall, but they could out-power a child, they thought. Or something the size of a child.

They placed their hand on the door handle, the other poised to flip the bolt.

From the other side of the door—only more silence.

FINDING THINGS AFTER YOU'RE GONE

"The physical world waits for me, but I do not
embrace it – for somewhere there's a long-lost
dream, and I must chase it."

Jennifer Brune, 1985-2012

I RUMMAGED THROUGH YOUR CLOSET WITHOUT MUCH HOPE OF finding what I was looking for. There wasn't much left, and others had found it all before I came home.

My eyes passed over the basket more than once, because it was falling apart and I didn't know it was yours. I didn't know you made things out of yarn and needles, but that's just one more thing I didn't know.

I didn't know, when I came home, wondering if you had a chance to read the story I started—the one we were going to write together—that the time was already past when we could have started something we would finish. Do you remember how we raced to finish our first books? The bet we made, that you collected? I forget what movie we went to see. I forget a lot these days. But I remember how you looked at the paper I handed you, and how you set it to the side.

So I took the basket and the yarn and the needles and brought it downstairs. Because you left so quickly, and there were so many things I didn't know, but if I finished this project, then maybe I, too, would be part of that secret life.

Did you know, the day before you left, that I had never met the sisters who came, fluttering around your bed like crows in the snow? They carried the Eucharist and they told me they had been on this journey with you. It was a journey I had had only glimpses of, postcards sent from a relative who remembers you even when you don't write back all the time.

You were patterning a rainbow, rows of colors and textures, and I stared at it until I put it away. Maybe you were smiling at me, when you put our story away. Maybe it was only ever my story, a comfort for me when I couldn't find a piece of you to take with me. Memory's a tricky thing.

Reading that book you sent me, I found these artifacts of you: veterinarian appointment slip for a dog who died before you did; your name in your handwriting on the frontispiece; unfolded silver gum wrapper. They marked your place and I re-read the words your eyes had cast over, and reveled in the uncharted territory beyond.

I found in the pile of mail on my desk a birthday card you wrote. Was it the chemistry set neurons that forgot to fire, forgot to send me this memento until it brought only pain and memory instead of congratulations?

But you did not leave me your shade. I found you sitting,

perched on the corner of the hutch in the living room, listening to music I hadn't forgotten to turn off.

It was an obscure album from an obscure band from the '90s. We had listened to them together, when I had an old car and a new license and every trip to the A&P was an adventure together.

And sometimes we would put some dollars together, and there would be a movie and a long, late drive through the Jersey night.

There was freedom and the promise of freedom, and I would light the way and you would hold the flame.

I stood in the dark of the living room for a long time, hoping these memories would drift away, recognizing in them the unfinished heat that comes in the wake of incomplete mourning.

You turned to me then, and the night left holes in your form, held together with shadows and the punk rock chords that fell like a lullaby around us.

TERMINAL LEAVE

IN THE LARGE ROOM IN THE SMALL HOME ON THE OUTSKIRTS OF Baghdad, our host cracked a bottle of tepid beer and poured us each half a shotglass full. The electricity in this suburb of the capital city was unreliable, and the family we were meeting with didn't own a working fridge. Still, they showed us hospitality serving us something they thought we would enjoy, so we drank the warm, flat lager and smiled through the conversation.

I would have preferred sticking to the water we carried, but our mission was to patrol through the towns surrounding our forward operating base, making nice with the locals and trying to convince them that we would be as not-inconvenient to their daily lives as possible. It was a futile task, because every now and then the bad guys used their houses for shelter and we'd have to go in and stomp around and piss everyone off. Or else, the redlegs would need to qualify with their Howitzers and we'd be paying some village chief a bunch of money to let us shoot up poor farmer's field. But it was our job as military police—escort the guys who knew how to talk nice to the locals, and make sure we didn't all get exploded or shot up in the process.

Don't get me wrong, I like beer. I've had a lot of fun, and done a few things I should probably regret, while drinking an adult beverage or four. For a long time I wanted to brew beer, but after telling people of my plans and listening to innumerable bad news stories about exploding bottles and corks launched with enough velocity to puncture walls, floors and ceilings, I had never quite gotten around to it. Especially living on Fort Bragg, with a husband who constantly worried about doing anything to the house that might end up in us paying massive cleaning fees when it came time to move out, I decided that discretion was the better part of valor, at least when it came to marriage and hobbies.

That wasn't a problem now. I had called home one morning after a long, boring night mission, the kind where nothing happened over a couple hundred miles of midnight desert road except a few loads of fuels, toothpaste, mail and vegetables got delivered to some remote base where soldiers couldn't otherwise get that stuff. It was about midnight in the states, and Jim had answered the phone groggy, voice faded and grainy with interrupted sleep. Halfway through the conversation, full of the inanities of long-term separation, I heard an unfamiliar ringtone. Jim swore, and then I heard another voice, feminine, delicate, answer a cell phone.

There had been a long silence, while I thought of all the joint parts of our life that were about to dissolve, and where he tried to think of something to say, and I hung up the receiver in the little plywood shack. My ten-minute time limit was up. I thought about what the woman might look like, if I knew her, if he was at her house when I called his cell phone—if he would get the Jeep and if I would get the dog. I ignored his emails for the last four months of the deployment, and when I stepped off the homecoming plane in the deep night humidity of a North Carolina summer, he was waiting there, divorce papers in hand. I signed them.

The call came at two in the morning, the time when any phone call is going to be bad news. I had turned the ringer down, but I was still a super light sleeper, and the vibrations of the phone against the wood of the nightstand jerked me awake, heart racing, hand dropping to the bed to search for my rifle.

I picked up the phone instead. It was my friend's number, a buddy from two deployments ago, but when I answered, the voice was strange.

"Who is this?" I asked.

"My name is Sara." The woman's voice was fragile, flavored with the Deep South. "Jackie had this number in his phone."

I knew immediately what had happened. My soldier had forgotten to change his contacts after moving on to another unit, and something had happened to him, and someone was calling because they thought I was still his squad leader.

"What's happened?" I asked.

"He's dead," she said, with the brutal honesty that comes when you don't know what to say. "He shot himself."

"Have..." I trailed off, trying to gather my thoughts. "Have you called the police?"

"Yes, they're here," she said. "I'm trying to call his unit."

So that's how I knew Specialist Jack Trimble was gone.

We had spent an entire deployment, him in the driver's seat of the truck, me in the TC seat as the team leader. He was always going on and on about fixing cars, racing dirtbikes and when we told him to shut up already about cars and dirtbikes, he had gone on to talk about his other favorite hobby, brewing beer. He had us groaning in pleasure and horror at the amount of beer he said was waiting in his basement, bottles and bottles of different ales and beers and stouts that would be aged to perfection when we got back. We hadn't seen or tasted a beer in months, and we alternately encouraged him and railed at him for riding us like that.

A few months after the 2:00 a.m. wakeup, I got another call. It was Sara again. I didn't want to answer the phone—I had missed the funeral, didn't send flowers, had spent most of the time crawling inside of bottles, trying to forget, while I sidestepped my way out of the Army. I hit 'Ignore' but she called back right away, so I answered it. She was cleaning up his stuff and had all of his brewing equipment and didn't want to throw it away or sell it—was it something I would be interested in?

So, here I was with an empty house and nothing but time and a serious urge to develop a drinking problem. I figured it was as good a time as any to get started. I told her I would take them.

I was living off-post now, out of the Army a couple of weeks, renting a house in a quiet part of the city. I had briefly thought about moving away from Fayettenam, but was still trying to find a job and was hoping to pick up something with some Army contractor or other. I couldn't seem to summon up a sense of urgency—I had about four months of terminal leave to live off of, and hadn't even hit the midway point yet.

"Excuse me?"

The voice was quiet, feminine, with a tinge of a familiar accent. I looked up and unconsciously reached for the pistol at my hip. I forced myself to relax and unclench my fingers. This drab creature in her black hijab and swathes of skirt and long-sleeved blouse was no threat.

"Yes?" I asked, wondering where she had come from.

She hesitated at the edge of the garage. I was working with the door open, and she had walked up the short concrete driveway to where I squatted, trying to fix my old mini-fridge in which I intended to eventually store the first batch of beer I brewed.

"Can I have some rice?" she asked.

I stared at her. I couldn't think of anything to say. "Uh ... how much?"

"Only two cups, I need," she said. "I will bring you, when I am done, dolma. You know? Dolma?"

I had a hard time understanding her. But I knew what dolma was. It was tasty, and I hadn't had any since getting back from Iraq. I had a random bag of rice in the pantry that I thought I remembered. "Hang on one second, I'll be right back."

She nodded and folded her hands in front of her. I dropped my tools next to the fridge and went inside. The house I was renting was a pretty modern design. The garage opened into a short space with a washing machine and dryer on one side and a closet on the other. I had stashed a load of old military crap in there, along with a bunch of dry foods I had brought from the old house. Most of it was rice and beans, things that required planning and cooking to use up. Those days I mostly went with microwave macaroni and cheese.

I gave her the rest of a ten-pound bag of white rice I had lying around. I wasn't going to use it. She took it with a strange relief and gratitude, which made me feel uncomfortable—too much thanks for something I was only going to throw away, after all.

"What are you doing?" she asked.

"Fixing a fridge," I said. "I'm planning on brewing a batch of koelsch. That's a kind of beer." I added the last to clear up the confusion I saw reflected in the twist of her mouth.

"You know how to do that?" she asked.

"Nah, but it can't be too hard," I said, with all the bravado of the neophyte. "I have a recipe."

"I mean the..." She trailed off. "Thank you for the rice."

And then she left and I didn't think any more of it until she came back with the dolma.

———

This time, she rang the doorbell and I invited her into the kitchen. I was getting ready to start boiling the first batch and I had already washed and sterilized all of the equipment three times. The instructions I had warned me very specifically, in no uncertain terms, not to allow any dirt or germs or bacteria onto the instruments or else the entire batch would be ruined and poisonous. The first time, I had repeated the sterilization process just to be sure. Then, I accidentally touched one of the many plastic tubes that belonged to the apparatus and dropped another one, and so I repeated the whole process all over again.

My fingers were clumsy around the instruments. I couldn't shake the feeling I was robbing the dead, even though I didn't think my buddy would mind I was carrying on his passion. I would think of him every time I cracked a cold one, but it was still creepy on some level.

The front door led into an open floor plan—family room sunk down one step on the right, open kitchen on the left, to the right a corridor that led back to a couple of bedrooms and to the extreme left, a small dining room. The decorating was generic. I had taken my credit card to Target and bought a bunch of new cheap stuff stained and bronzed to look like old cheap stuff.

"Come on in," I said. "Have a seat."

"I only have ten minutes," she said.

"Let me make you some tea," I said.

She was wearing the same outfit she had worn previously, but the hijab did not obscure her entire face and I saw surprise in her expression when I got out the tea set I had brought back from Iraq. It was one of the few things I had taken from the old house.

"Thank you," she said.

She placed the dolma on the small kitchenette table and seated herself in one of the low chairs. I moved some paperwork and old bills off the surface and put them on the counter. Now, she could see my cheap linen tablecloth with the daisy pattern I had bought thinking the bright pinks, yellows and greens would cheer me up.

I put two small plates down as the water boiled. Her gaze took in the house, lingering over the mad scientist assortment of pipes and tubing and containers that littered the counter.

"Is that for your kass?" she asked.

"Koelsch? Yes," I said. I measured out tablespoonsful of granular brown sugar, tipping them into the tiny tea glasses. Once the water boiled, I would steep the tea—leaves I still had from deployment—and then pour it over the sugar.

She didn't say anything else.

"It's my first time trying it out," I said, to fill the silence that quickly grew awkward.

She nodded.

"My family is from central Germany," I told her. "When I

was younger, my mom used to tell us we had relatives there, still, who owned a brewery. They make koelsch—Kupper Koelsch."

I told the same story to the guy at the homebrewing store up in Raleigh. He seemed mildly interested when I explained, as I did to my visitor, that all my life I had taken a sort of half-pride in the fact that my family was in the brewing business. It was only when I got older and the Internet was invented that I finally got around to searching the family lore and found out that the pride and joy of the American Kuppers was actually one of the worst-rated koelsches in all of Germany, and indeed the entire world. When I told the guy at the store that I wanted to see if I could do better to redeem the family name to myself, I was only half-joking.

"Very good," she said, as I finished my story and the tea, placing a cup in front of her. I smelled the waft of mint and black tea and sat across from her. After two months, she was my first visitor.

"When it's done, you should come over and try some," I said.

"I cannot," she said, embarrassed. "It is ... *haram*."

There was another awkward silence. I was batting a thousand today.

"What's your name?" I asked.

"Safiya," she said.

"Nice to meet you, Safiya," I said. "My name is Rebecca."

She sipped her tea. "I don't want to keep you."

I shrugged. "I'm not in a hurry."

And I wasn't. I had a bunch of ingredients in my fridge I didn't understand and pile of equipment on my counter with forbidding names like "siphon hose" and "hydrometer" and "mash paddle." I had a book and a sheet of paper printed out from the Internet.

She set the tea glass back down on the table. "I must go. My husband will be home soon."

And then I suspected that maybe she wasn't really supposed to be hanging out, sipping tea in some stranger's house.

"Well, I don't have that problem anymore," I said.

She frowned.

"No husband," I said and tried to laugh it off. She frowned again.

"I must go."

"Thanks for the dolma," I said. "I'll get your dish back to you."

She nodded without saying anything and left.

I stared at the table. The dolma sat, twelve little pieces of chicken and rice wrapped snugly in their grape leaves. They were still warm. I picked one up in the first three fingers of my right hand and brought it to my mouth, inhaling the scents of spices and meat. I bit down, gently, cupping my other hand under my chin to catch any stray bits.

The taste shuddered through me. I put the rest of the roll in my mouth and chewed slowly. I felt a curious tightening in my chest and my throat dried. It got harder to chew and it was only when I buried my face in my hands, feeling the wetness on my cheeks, that I realized I was crying. I choked it down and wiped my eyes. Breathing deeply I stood up, went to the sink, turned on the cold water and washed my face. I stood there with the water running over my hands for a long time.

A couple days after that, I washed all the equipment again. I still hadn't started the batch, and I was worried that dust or dirt might have gotten on it, sitting on the counter like that.

This time, I refused to let myself worry or think. I told myself, I wasn't the first one to try homebrewing, and clearly many other people before me had attempted and succeeded with this fine kit and recipe, and so it was time to quit crying about it and just do the damn thing.

The recipe kit I bought from the store had all the ingredients pre-measured and sorted, which was convenient. As per the instructions, I boiled the water and crushed grains, using my buddy's thermometer to make sure the heat held steady right between the upper and lower temperature delimitations. I had a moment of panic when I grasped the pot handles with my bare hands and had to quickly rummage through a couple of drawers to find pot holders, and then another moment when I realized the recipe called for me to rinse the mixture with water that was already at a high temperature and I hadn't even started the heat under that pot.

Eventually I got the malt and different kinds of hops into the same pot and boiling at what I hoped was the perfect temperature, and that the missteps and hesitations would not permanently damage the process. I felt less as if I were cooking something than that I was playing around with a chemistry set, especially when I went to pour the wort into the fermentation vessel and then realized that I needed another couple of gallons of water—this time cold water—and some apparatus called an airlock. By now I had my laptop on the counter trying to identify which pieces of equipment were which. I was sweating and angry and cursing myself, the recipe, the guy at the homebrewing store and my buddy for making it seem so easy.

The next part of the recipe was simple—wait for seven days. I left the fermentation vessel or, as I called it, the fucking pail, on the floor of my kitchen. The unfermented beer would remain at the right temperature inside and I knew that if I put it outside in the garage I would forget about it and there would go the twenty bucks I spent on the kit and recipe, and the entire morning of work.

I needed to do something I knew how to do, something that would be easy for me, mindless. I decided to clean my guns.

I have three pistols and a shotgun. I keep them locked up, unloaded, when I'm drinking. Jack wasn't the only one who found it too easy to reach for one when he was mired in low places. But now they were sitting in inanimate pieces across the daisy-patterned tablecloth, and I had a half-empty bottle of Shiner bock to keep me company as I wiped away the remnants of the morning's range practice. My hands were covered in carbon and cleaning lubricant when the doorbell rang.

I left greasy fingerprints on the shiny doorknob, opening it to find my new friend Safiya. She stepped into the house quickly, moving to hide behind me.

"Is everything all right?" I asked.

"Yes, fine," she said. "I need my dish."

"Okay," I said. "Come on in."

I looked out on the street, casting a glance about to see if there was anyone following her, or any other reason for her strange entrance. Not finding anything, I closed the door and went back into the kitchen. I found her sitting at the dinette, hands in her lap, looking at the gun parts scattered across the tabletop.

"Would you like some tea?" I asked. "I still have to wash your dish."

"That's okay, I can just take it and go," she said, but her hurry was belied by the fact she sat down.

"No, no, please, it's not a problem," I said. "Let me start some water to boil."

"Thank you," she said.

And then we once again ran out of things to say to each other, so I made the tea, gave her a cup, and pulled the empty dolma dish out of the refrigerator. I had been snacking at odd intervals, pulling one after the other out of the ceramic container with my fingers, not stopping to re-heat them or use a fork and knife. Once done, I had left the empty container in there along with some rapidly-souring milk and an empty cheese wrapper.

"What do these look like?" she asked. "When they are one piece?"

She had a curious way of speaking, like her English vocabulary was limited, so she had to think of new ways to say things.

"They're just pistols," I told her. "Like you see on TV."

"What it feels to hold one in your hands?" she asked.

She reminded me of my own curiosity the first time I had held my first gun. Unlike me, she kept her fingers to herself, wrapping them around the tea glass.

I put down the dish in the warm, soapy water, and dried my hands on a paper towel. Picking up some of the pieces, I put the spring back in the barrel of the Sig Sauer P220, racked the slide and locked it back. I handed it toward her. "You want to take a look?"

She shook her head. "No, thank you. For women, that is *haram*."

I refrained from stating the obvious, that I was a woman, and that it obviously wasn't that forbidden, and also that I had seen other Middle Eastern women using guns, but I'm used to operating around people with radically different opinions than I about what women should and should not do. And not all of those people are from the Middle East.

"What does it feel like?" she asked. "To hold that?"

I told her, the first time is strange, and that you should never get so comfortable with them that you forget what they're capable of, but the truth is, I've become more than comfortable with them. I told her they were easy to buy in Texas, although not so much here. She didn't say anything, but I thought I caught a look on her face. She put her hand to her cheek.

"Oh hey," I said. "I finally started the koelsch."

"It smells," she said.

"I guess it does."

She caught my frown. "I'm sorry, I meant I smell it."

"Yeah, it's kind of distinctive," I said, although I couldn't smell anything except CLP from the cleaning kit. We sat, again in silence, which was almost growing comfortable. I finished putting together the rest of the pistols, nestling them in their hard, black cases, closing them up for the next time I ventured to the range.

Someone pounded on the door. Safiya jumped, spilling tea on the tablecloth. She said something in Arabic.

"It's okay," I said. "The tablecloth's machine washable."

She shook her head. "I am sorry."

"Excuse me a minute," I said, and went to answer the bell.

When I opened the door, I didn't recognize the man standing there, but I knew it was Safiya's husband. He was about my height, five-seven, in a suit with shiny shoes.

"Come home, now," he said.

I stared at him, but then Safiya pushed her way past me, holding the dripping dish against her chest, the water staining the dark fabric of her shirt.

I watched, the uncomfortable observer to this domestic drama, as he turned and stalked off my porch, making his angry way down the wide suburban sidewalk. She followed after him, hurrying to stay at his heels. I shook my head. I had seen this sort of situation before, but hadn't expected it to drop onto my front porch or come sit in my kitchen. I wondered if I should say something, or maybe get the number of someone for her to call next time I saw her, but then the self-centeredness I'd been wallowing in for the past couple of months reasserted itself and I simply shrugged and made a note to try to bring it up in conversation if she ever rang the doorbell again.

The directions I had said to bottle the koelsch after fourteen days, and then to wait an additional two weeks before drinking it. I decided I would keep half the bottles in the mini-fridge for those two weeks, and keep the other half stored at room temperature, to see which ones came out better. My buddy had insulated his basement and kept it at a carefully climate-controlled sixty degrees, but I wasn't about to renovate my garage when I was only renting the house and wasn't sure if I was even going to ever make another batch of beer.

I spent the time puttering around the house, rearranging my resume, thinking about sending it out to a couple of places. The job market wasn't as bad where I was, but there still weren't a plethora of open hires. I toyed with the idea of investing in a piece of land and starting a business, but I couldn't think of anything I wanted to do badly enough to deal with the heartburn of trying to be a small business owner in this economy.

The day after I bottled my first homebrew, I decided to

skip a day of job searching and head to the range. I pulled my pistol cases out from the top of my closet and brought them into the kitchen. Setting them on the table, I opened each one to make sure I had all of my magazines and cleaning equipment.

My Springfield XDS was not in its case.

I had a fun time after that, calling the police, reporting that the .45-caliber, easily concealable firearm was inexplicably vanished from my collection. They sent an officer to take my report, a young kid fresh out of the academy who clearly hadn't been assigned to many challenging cases yet because he tried hard to think of a lot of good, probing questions to ask for his investigation. I told him that no, I hadn't taken the guns out since the last time I went to the range a month ago. Yes, I was the only one in the house in all that time. And here, I caught the whiff of a pitying look. And no, I had no idea who took the thing. And here, the look turned suspicious.

He took my paperwork, made a copy of my concealed carry permit and the receipt of purchase, noted the serial number, and told me to have a nice day. I decided to take his advice, forego the range, and spend the rest of the afternoon drinking on the back porch.

As it turned out, the bottles I had put on the shelf in the garage tasted better than the ones that had aged in the mini-fridge. I made a solemn, solitary ceremony of the first tasting, chilling the shelf-aged beer in the refrigerator, cracking the bottles with my special bottle opener with the military police crest on it, carefully pouring a small taste of each into two small glasses.

I brought the samples out to the back porch. The first one I sipped was the fridge-aged. I held it in my mouth, rolling the light amber liquid around my tongue and gums. It tasted hoppy, but tart, and stronger than normal beer. I swallowed it, then poured the rest of it on the grass. A strange bitterness lingered in the back of my throat, coating my tongue.

"For you, buddy," I said to myself.

I did the same with the other glass. This one tasted ... better. The aroma was sharper, and the taste lingered longer. When I swallowed, the aftertaste burned like satisfaction down my throat. I poured the rest of that glass out, too, an offering to some obscure household god. I got a kick out of imagining Jack, and his horrified reaction at the waste of a good beer.

The night was cool, summer fading fast into a reluctant autumn. I still perspired as I sat out on the back porch, a gift of the North Carolina humidity. But it wasn't unpleasant. I finished the two bottles I had opened, thinking about my buddy, thinking a lot of what-if type thoughts about things that might have happened. It was the sort of night when you don't need anyone around, because the ghosts of those who aren't there are more present than any living person would be.

I fell asleep in my camp chair. Around midnight, I jerked awake, trying to make sense of what I was hearing. Commotion and gunshots from a neighbor's house—not the first time I'd ever been thus awakened in the middle of the night, but that was in post housing. I thought I had left that behind me when I moved off the base. I set my beer bottles upright on the back porch, went back inside and called the police. I was loading rounds back into my Sig when my doorbell echoed through the house.

I opened the door and Safiya stood on my front porch, my gun still in her hand. She was real calm, her face unmoving, betraying no emotion. She wasn't wearing her hijab. I led her into the kitchen without a word. She sat down, placing the gun carefully on the table. I left it there.

Going in the cabinet, I took down a glass. I paused.

"You want a beer?" I asked, although I thought I already knew the answer.

"No, thank you," she said. "It is *haram*."

I got some ice cubes and water from the tap and gave her the glass. We waited together for the police to show up.

HOLES

IT WAS SUBTLE, AND I DIDN'T REALIZE IT AT FIRST.

I can't remember why I was going through the pile of old photos—probably on another Marie Kondo-inspired cleaning and decluttering kick. I go through those every once in a while, pulling everything out and putting it in a pile and maybe organizing one or two things ... and then getting distracted and forgetting about the pile until it's time to go to bed and I shift it to the floor, where it stays for another couple of weeks or months.

The faces looking out of this picture were somewhat faded, but this was a properly developed photo from a film negative, not a computer printout, and so even though it was over three decades old, I could still make out everyone's face. Their hair. Eyes. Glasses for some. Braces for a few unlucky others. We had all mostly gotten over that phase of life, but there I was, back row, right in the center, smiling a grin full of metal. My orthodontist made a lot of money off my parents, with my mouth all cluttered and out of whack.

I could barely remember any of the other kids' names. We'd spent the entire summer at camp, swore to stay besties forever, said we'd write every day. That hadn't even lasted a week. I'd never sent a letter. I'd gotten one—a postcard from Jennifer Anne. She'd sent one to everyone, but I never wrote back and never received another letter. I'd looked her up on social media a few years ago to find that she'd married and had two kids before passing. Cancer, I think.

Looking at the photo, I couldn't remember where she'd stood. Was that her on the end? I seem to remember them putting her on the end. But none of the kids on the ends looked like her.

I put the photo on my dresser, thinking that I'd eventually frame it and add it to the collection of photos on the filing cabinet in my office.

That's probably why I noticed the next one so much more quickly. I was organizing my underwear into neat little rolls, just like in the book, folding and rolling and stacking so I could easily see at a glance what I had. Oddly satisfying. I looked up at the photo and paused, my sturdy cotton panties dangling from my hand.

Because there was a hole in the middle of the photo.

Someone had been in the photo, and they weren't there now. Unlike Jennifer Anne, I remembered exactly who had been standing there, because he had been standing in front of me. I, as the tallest, was center back. He was two inches shorter than me, with a personality like a big, goofy magnet. Everyone had wanted to be Matt's friend, and he was the kind of guy who would return the friendship. I'd had the biggest crush, and had been so excited that he was positioned exactly in front of me.

And now, he wasn't there.

The tiniest suspicion started to form. I dropped the underwear and closed the drawer, picked up my phone and opened social media. Matt had been one of the first guys I connected with when social media came out. We had a ton of mutual friends from high school. And now, as I scrolled through my feed, every one of them was expressing a torrent of sadness.

"Matt, we miss you, can't believe you're gone."

"All the best to Matt and his family—he was a true light."

"RIP Matt; can't believe you're gone."

Plus, lots of emojis and gifs. People in their forties love sprinkling emojis and gifs into everything, even mourning posts.

I added my own message to the list—*My condolences to your family* *sad face emoji* *heart emoji*—and closed my phone. I never did finish organizing my underwear drawer.

Matt and Jennifer Anne weren't the first people my age to pass. The first person I'd known was a friend from college who passed away in a car accident when we were in our mid-twenties. Since then, it wasn't a common occurrence to lose a friend, but it wasn't unknown, either.

Still ... Jennifer Anne had passed away a few months ago. Then Matt. I wondered if the same thing would happen, if someone else's face and body and those crazy clothes we all thought were so on trend would all fade from the photo like they never existed.

The answer was yes.

I didn't know the next person to fade, and try as I could to search social media, to connect with mutual friends online, I couldn't figure out who they were, or if they had died. But two weeks later there was the hole, nonetheless, where a teenage girl had once stood on the top row.

After that, that holes started showing up faster and faster. At first, they disappeared about a week apart. Some of them, I could track down. Find out what happened. Car accident. Suicide. Military service. Heart attack. Nothing out of the ordinary. Nothing connected. Just ... life. And death.

The last few, though. Those have been coming faster and faster. Six days apart. Five days. Then, three holes, three days apart.

I see what's coming. And I don't know if I mind so much the fact that it *is* coming, as I mind the fact that it's happening now. I always thought if I was going to go out in a blaze of glory, it would be a righteous party and a bender of truly epic proportions. But nobody's leaving their house now. I've gotten used to this strange hermit existence. Even if I wanted to go out, I can't imagine trying to explain to a friend why I wouldn't be worried about catching anything.

I've been staring at this photo so long, the final figure just melted away, another hole, leaving me standing there at the top and center of the risers. I forgot I had that pair of Chuck Taylors, the red ones I'd saved up for, so proud of them, wearing them with those super baggy jeans and that flannel shirt.

Perhaps I won't fade. Perhaps I won't be just another hole in the photograph.

I'll find out soon enough.

THE PEACEMAKER

THE NOVA WALKS INTO THE ROOM. THEN HE GLIDES INTO THE room. The next time, he tries coming in the window. The producer wants to make it look as natural as possible, so they do it a couple more times from a couple of different angles.

Then it's my turn. For this episode, they've dressed me in what my PR guy tells me is my signature outfit. Black dress slacks, black sports coat, white button-down shirt and skinny black tie, nicely contrasted by the scruffy black Chuck Taylors and about a half a day of forgetting to shave or brush my teeth after the last beer.

At least the shoes are comfortable. I walk in, picturing myself in slo-mo, like a reject extra in some Quentin Tarantino film. Which would probably pay more. We do it a couple times, and I can't even pretend to be interested in what lies behind door number two.

The next take, the guy with the Steadicam gets right up in my face. They're going for the reaction shot. Something in that room was put there just for me. I shrug and open the front door to the house I share with five other people who wish they were somewhere else.

Jack.

Did I say his name out loud? I don't think so. My mouth is too full of spit and bile.

Nevertheless, my former partner turns his head in my general direction. His DAC is sort of listing to one side. They're a bitch like that, always sliding around no matter how much effort you make with the straps and clips and duct tape.

DAC—digital access camera. I'm acutely aware of the silence surrounding us, and the ice that threatens to well up in the cavern between us. I got nothing. Somewhere some editor is cussing me out. The last time I saw Jack, everyone thought he was going to die.

That sudden anger, the flash of pure fury that always seemed to come from a deep, cold place in me, veils my eyes momentarily. I come back to myself on the back porch, staring silently at the ocean, just the tiniest hint of frost glistening on the wrought iron railing. I don't know how I got out here, but the camera followed me, and I guess I'm going to make the highlights reel this week.

Wilmington Beach. A second-rate vacation spot of some local fame. Chances are if you live in North Carolina or West Virginia, your grandparents spent at least one vacation here.

It's a sort of cut-rate picturesque type of place, which is how the producers are able to afford the big house on the shore. Not big enough to give us enough space, but enough to ensure that the week's conflict can be featured in as many different rooms as possible. Viewers get bored apparently. Our viewers more than most.

I'm still not sure why people are watching this shit. None of us are famous anymore. The house, the show, the prize—

this is just how far we've fallen. A couple of us do guest spots on other shows, but the rest, like me, were just C-List enough to get offered a big house, annoying roommates, and a chance to give America a front seat to our inevitable decline.

After the cameras go off, the producer, a kid who introduces himself by the Hollywood moniker of The Big Show, tells me that Jack is going to be staying. He's our new housemate. But don't worry, because he'll normally be very heavily chemically sedated. I have nothing to do with that.

Or maybe I did.

I head into the kitchen. Wolf-Boy's at the grill. He outgrew the juvenile tag twenty pot-filled years ago, but it's one of those things. You get tagged, and what are you going to do? Not like The Big Show—who everyone except the guy who rolls the credits calls Bob. He picked his own nickname and good luck trying to make it stick when you do that. Sometimes you work a brand and sometimes that's not what happens.

My hands are clammy. I'm not good at this—the adrenaline starts to rush, and then I want the ice to come, and then I remember where I am and get a beer from the fridge and try to ignore my former partner sitting across the house from me, eyes fixed on no particular place, DAC just about falling off the end of his temple on his flimsy elastic strap.

"You want a burger?" Wolf-Boy's voice has a growl to it. He smokes about a pack and a half a day. He does it to sound cool. And maybe die quicker.

"No." The beer will hold me over until I heat up some of yesterday's Thai delivery.

I'm more interested in whatever the hell Venus is doing. American Venus. Her looks earned her that particular appellation, and the feminists had a field day with it. She is a cheery beacon of love. All the time. At first I thought it would wear off.

I sit and watch. She hums to herself as she bedazzles her DAC with black and gold rhinestones and little skull stickers. Wolf-Boy brings his slab of steak dinner to the table, seared on one side and mostly bleeding all over. He has this habit of playing his role to the hilt, but there are no cameras here, at least none that we know of.

"Wolfie." Her voice is as sweet as her face. "You know I'm vegetarian."

"It's my dinner, babe," he says. "You don't like it, go glue your little doily in the living room."

The rush of her anger under the cheer is manna from heaven, hot nectar from an American goddess. I feel the familiar itching in my palms, and clench my fists, squelching the desire to offer her the opportunity to bask in the calm that I can bring. She looks up and smiles. I don't know if she realizes how close I came to getting kicked out already. Or maybe she does, and that's why she's smiling.

Venus smiles and starts to hum again, the pitch way, way off. Wolf-Boy's ears twitch in agony and then I'm treated to the molasses hate that burns its way through his lanky form.

Jack sits in the corner, nodding in time to the tuneless song she continues to sing. Gracelessly, I push my chair back. Pouring the rest of the beer out, I toss the empty bottle in the sink and stalk out of the room. I know that later we'll have to "talk" about this little "incident" and how it made the Lovely Venus feel, but for now I have to get out of here.

I'm standing on the porch again. Jack comes up, uncomfortably close. I can feel him breathing on my cheek. Something is rotten deep in him, something that won't be solved by brushing his teeth. It's the chemicals they have him on. They've reached all through him, folding him into their bioengineered embrace. His eyes try hard to focus and I think I see recognition in there, but it could be my imagination and I don't really want to think about what happened. I wish I hadn't tossed the beer.

I can't say I was surprised to see him here. I'd wondered when he would show up. They'd been bringing in some of the other sidekicks every couple of weeks. No one expected any of them to win, but they might get one of us to break the code. If that happened, their prize money would be just as real, and they'd probably need it more than we did. A guy like the Nova, he'd been in cheesy martial arts movies since the '90s and with a little Miracle Hair could keep going another decade or so.

"Jack. You in there big guy?"

My voice startles my former partner. Instead of focusing on me, though, he cranes his head to look up at the weather-beaten wood planks of the ceiling. I leave him standing there and head down to the ocean. It's freezing this time of year, and the water feels like heaven on my bare feet.

I made the big time when Strongman had his break with reality on a platform at Grand Central Station. One moment he had been fighting something with way too many tentacles that had slithered up one of the tunnels from the East River, the next he was demolishing anything that looked at him sideways. And given that he was shouting something about the walls having eyes, there wasn't much left of that venerable landmark by the time I heard the call over the scanner.

I got out there in time to drop him in his tracks before he finally brought the roof down on himself and about 200 other tourists, commuters and groupies who had rushed to see their hero beat down some tentacle ass. That's not to say there weren't casualties.

Prior to that, I had been working as a cop. It wasn't quite an alter ego, since nobody was quite sure what I could do. Even me.

After that, I took a couple gigs in international security, corporate negotiations. Wasn't as flashy as some, but seemed a good fit. Every once in a while, I got caught up in something the heavy hitters had going on, but mostly I had my steady gig at the NYPD.

Jack volunteered to be my partner once it became obvious that I was something more than a cop. We didn't call them sidekicks. Partner was better. He was there to keep me down to earth, to call me back whenever the ice tried to lead me too far. I tasted the emotions of the crowd, or the negotiators, or the nemesis *du jour*, and encased them in the cold quiet of calm order.

They called it The Peace, and me The Peacemaker. I remember shivering in the pleasure of its path through my fingers.

End of the week. Time for the "house meeting." We sit and throw one-liners at each other, competing to see who can get the prized spot of rage and potential loss of control that will be cut into the trailer for that week's show.

I dread these things. They wreck my calm.

As I suspected, Venus launches into a rant about the respect for personal life choices, to be free from others' tyranny toward lower species—here Wolf-Boy growls, as if worried she is including him in that category. She probably is.

The Nova interrupts. "Not everyone can live on wheatgrass and dingleberries."

"I don't think that's a very helpful remark." Venus is conspicuous in her choice of "you" language. "It makes me feel very hurt when others don't respect Mother Nature."

"It's a fucking cow," says Wolf-Boy. "The only thing she was mother of was about a dozen calves they bred from her until it was time to turn her into hamburger."

The emotions spark back and forth. I struggle to stay abreast of them, holding myself above the waves. I sense the guy with the Steadicam inching closer.

"Back off, Cletus." I stand up and take a breath. I get ignored.

The Nova jumps back into the conversation, raising his voice. Venus gets a hurt face on, lowers her voice, puts the pout in her lower lip. Wolf-Boy lights up another cigarette like he's not supposed to.

I sit back down and watch Jack as he tracks back and forth, following the pitch and tone if not the conversation. It must be like someone is randomly turning a volume knob in his brain.

"Listen up, people." I stand again and raise my hands, a neutral gesture, completely misinterpreted. Venus squeals and cowers. Wolf-Boy leaps straight into the air and comes down behind the low partition that separates the living room from the kitchen space. He crouches by the refrigerator.

Cletus gets closer, and I have an audience of one bright staring glass eye. There is a moment in which I can already hear the cheesy swell of foreboding strings they are going to layer over this moment. I put my hands down, force myself to draw the calm back in.

"We just have to work together." It's definitely an anticlimactic moment. Venus sits back on the couch and readjusts her cleavage.

Wolf-Boy tries to get something started again, but then Jack wanders off, Venus gets a call on her cell—which was supposed to be on silent—and the meeting kind of drifts away. It doesn't make for exciting television, but what are you going to do?

The Big Show is not happy, standing in the living room, berating everyone unfortunate to have been caught inside when he showed up. Our ratings are dropping, which means commercial revenues are down. Way down. I think they're starting to use some of the prize money for craft services. This week, especially, it seems that the show failed to generate any controversy; it had generally failed to spur anything online. Even hatred. They should tape this guy's rant. It might help perk up the numbers.

While Bob wracks his brain, I stand on the back porch, watching the ocean. Drink a beer. The house grows uncomfortably small and quiet. When the cameras aren't here, I prefer to stay outside.

I could have told him why his show was diving. People don't watch us because we're hip or cool or they wish they were us or had our problems. They watch to wait for one of us to lose control, for it to be THAT moment, caught live on cameras.

The laws against use of our special talents are pretty strict. I'm sorry to say I was the reason most of them were enacted in the knee jerk legislative reaction that always seems to accompany the actions of one disturbed individual.

That was me, just for the record. It seems that the calming influence I can project, both the light waves of cool collectiveness and the intense ice shards of frozen watchfulness—the physical manifestations they called The Peace—leave more than a small piece of themselves inside everyone they touched.

At first it wasn't that noticeable. There were a few people who never got over their PTSD from the Strongman incident, just kind of sat back in their figurative rocking chairs and let the rest of their lives happen to them.

Then there were a few other things that happened. Strange growths found on some of the internal organs of various suicide victims in the City. Public Health had a fine time alarming the public with fears of some new biological weapon. Nobody could put it together, though, and like all the other amorphous threats of bio-warfare that filtered out of the media, it got tucked back into some Internet graveyard, moving out of the way to make room for the latest paparazzi shot of Venus and her Beau of the Week.

I could have noticed the change in Jack, but we weren't that close. I mean, we were, but he had come to me a cold, reserved man, the kind who finds it easy to control what few emotions he has.

We were ideal for each other. When it got hard to be around other people, when the taste-the-rainbow waves of pain and anger threatened to become overwhelming rather than sustaining, he was there to pull me back on dry land.

He came with me on that call. It was The Rager, our friendly, local recidivist. The first time we faced each other, he had left more than one scorch mark on a sensitive part of my anatomy. The papers loved our duels—Fire and Ice they liked to call it—and published great big color pictures of The Rager and The Peacemaker, duking it out with some iconic NYC scenery in the background.

Unfortunately for the City, I had been growing steadily, stealthily more powerful, and he had been getting more angry and powerful. Our final showdown was on its way, just like you see in the comic book mashup movies.

It was going to be an epic battle, but then it happened outside the wrought-iron fence walls of a high-school parking lot. That day The Peace rose quickly, violently, and when the dust settled, The Rager was nothing more than crystallized flesh and bone.

They finally figured out that Public Health crisis. The same growths found on the suicide victims matched exactly The Rager's petrified flesh. And the flesh on the six students and three teachers killed outright, standing within the shadow of the blast.

The suicides came after. Other people—just weren't the people they had been before.

Jack ended up in an institution, his attempt foiled by the misfire of his service revolver. From that time, harsh chemicals and fluorescent lights had kept him in the land of the living. Even if what he was doing wasn't quite that.

It's getting dark. The tide is pulling back from the shore. Three of the last beers in the house sit on the table next to me. It's been a couple hours, but it's cold enough outside to keep them chilled. I debate going back in the house. I could spend the night out here, with the cold as my welcome companion.

Better than the house. Jack's taken to roaming the halls the past couple nights. I get insomnia bad. My brain can't shut down for a couple hours after everyone goes to bed, too full from processing their offerings of jealousy and petty hate.

I can't stand to see him. Not that I feel guilty. Sometimes I do. Every time I go near, he turns to look at me, as if realizing he knows me. But the memory slips away every time his brain gets close to grasping hold of recognition.

The screen door slams behind me with more force than I intended. I pause, holding my breath, waiting to see if I woke anyone. I don't hear any sudden shuffling or movement, so I settle down and go to put the empty bottles in the sink. It's a habit that pisses off the American Venus, who thinks all beer bottles should be placed in the recycling, but it's dark and I don't want to.

I stand at the sink, the last bottle still in my hand, looking out the window over the dark sand. The full moon casts a path across the ocean. With the breeze coming in the screen door, I can just barely still hear the waves.

The slightest hint of frost forms at my fingers, leaving faint tracks across the glass bottle. I try to hold in the dark calm, but there are no cameras here, no prying housemates. Only myself and the night and The Peace.

"Mike?"

The bottle slips from my hand and lands with a surprisingly dull thump in the metal sink. I turn to see Jack, standing in the shadows at the edge of the room. His eyes are more focused. His head drifts around. I realize he is looking for the all-seeing eye. There is nothing but the dark.

He comes closer. I lean back against the sink, but he stops a few feet away this time. His eyes rest somewhere below mine, still unable to make eye contact.

"I remember you."

Jack's voice is loud in the room. I wince and lower my voice to reply. "Do you, partner?" I didn't realize my voice would come out so brittle.

My attempt to get him to whisper has no effect. He says in a normal tone: "I remember." I wait for him to continue, but he can't.

Jack drops his gaze and looks around. Carefully, almost delicately he pulls a chair from the table and drags it to where he can see out the door into the gloom over the water. He sits there for a while. I wait for him to say something else, but that's all he's got for me.

I move to stand behind him, my hands resting on his shoulders. It's a curiously intimate gesture for two men who have not seen each other in years, and who were never close, but it doesn't feel awkward. He reaches up to my hand, clasping it in his.

There is a jolt as his pain washes over me. There is something dead under the pain, as if it, too, had metastasized under the touch of The Peace. The calm starts to rise in me again. My hand grows cold, and the ice grows cold and clear. I step forward to stand beside him.

Jack looks up at me. I know he can feel The Peace like an offering in my skin. A light flashes deep behind his eyes. Just for a second, I wonder if I miscalculated, but then he is gone under the ice.

I've tried, but I can't do it. My ability to accept that something I almost had grasped—a chance for recognition, a chance to do the right thing in the world—had slipped irreconcilably away. I can't say when it happened, but I suspect it began when I put the Strongman down on the cold filthy marble of the Grand Central Station.

Revelations that occur after midnight and before the sun rises are not to be trusted. We are more prone to act because we cannot see an end to the despair, to the blackness that settles down, makes itself part of something that cannot be excised without losing something important part of yourself.

The Peace rises in me, the cold heart of its promise begging to slip from my hold. Through the velvet silence, I feel the dim threads of dream hate, anger, worry, jealousy and just the slightest amount of love, courtesy of Venus, seep through the night.

I reach out and grasp the metal railing, the cold leaching itself into my palms, to be met by the slow, encroaching tide of ice. Questing out, I push the shadows of silent canyons through the fragile modern spaces of the house.

A sigh drifts up, the only sign that life still clings to its idea, if not its fleshly reality. There is a sound like coughing, and then I'm alone.

My bag holds a few necessities, and I don't mind helping myself to the keys to one of The Big Show's shiny cars. I have a long way to go. I was never much of a hero; now I realize that was never my calling. All I can offer is a final sort of Peace.

AND OUT COME THE WOLVES

NICKY HAD LEARNED A NEW CUSS WORD. YOU'D THINK THE KID'S vocabulary would have already developed a wide selection, but he was really young and really new, and was having fun trying them all out. He was intent on showing us how cool he was, finding a way to insert it in every other sentence. Every time he said it, he would pause and flinch for just the briefest of moments and then bluff his way to the next potential usage. At first, it was kind of funny, but there comes a point when enough's enough.

Big Mike abruptly got to that point. Gently laying his rifle on the worktable, he cuffed Nicky upside the head, mussing the kid's hair with his thick, greasy palm.

"Knock it off, Nicky," he said. "Or I'mma write your mother, tell her you got a dirty mouth."

The threat worked, and Nicky bowed his head back over the innards of his own rifle. The backs of his ears were bright red as he scrubbed away with the cleaning rag and re-oiled the parts of the weapon.

Probably forty years ago this had been the main drag of a small town in the upper West corner of New Jersey, but now it belonged to the Protectorate. An old library, the ruins of the bar we'd taken over for our common area, and the remains of a hardware store bordered the asphalt square. We were sitting around someone's old dinner table, now a work area piled high with cleaning kits and disassembled weapons parts, enjoying the dawn breaking around the end of our shift. The tent shade covering us made a pleasant flapping sound as a morning breeze drifted through.

One last swipe with a rag, and I fitted the bolt back in the chamber of my rifle. I wiped my hands as clean as they were going to get and fitted the barrel back into the receiver, locked the bolt back, and got ready to turn the weapon back into the arms room. It had been a long shift, even on a fine spring night when the weather was warming and the nights were shrinking. I was ready for bed.

"Night, Minions," I said. "Nicky—keep practicing."

Big Mike distractedly waved his middle finger at me. "Don't forget, CO wanted to see you," he said without looking up.

I hadn't forgotten, but I'd hoped the squad had. Plausible deniability.

I switched one hope for another and thought maybe by dragging my feet the CO might have gone home for the day. Usually the arms room is good for at least half an hour, but this morning the kids working behind the security bars were the very models of bushy-tailed efficiency and I was out in ten minutes. Some days more than others I truly regretted the vast apocalyptic turn of events that wiped out three-quarters of the world's population, taking with it the last cup of coffee.

Hope might spring eternal, but strange how luck never seemed to accompany it. My CO was sitting behind my desk in the office I shared with the other squad leaders. She was a lean woman, whip tough, her graying blonde hair cropped short and severe. Her frown, along with her pristine, sharply-pressed uniform contrasted with the casual attitude with which she propped her booted feet up on a stack of reports I was going to get around to submitting.

"Bag anything tonight?"

"No joy," I replied. She wasn't going to rag on me about the bag count. Behind her, on the wall, hung the evidence of my squad's eager beaver attitudes toward killing biodapts and destroying their universe. We killed things people didn't even know existed.

"You guys have had a run of slow shifts the past couple of weeks," she said.

So maybe she *was* going to rag on me about the bag count. "It's been—a little slow out there." I caught myself just in time from saying the "Q" word. Everyone knew saying that word would guarantee the next shift would bring snarly, nasty beasts to the walls.

"Huh." The CO thought about that for a second or two, then swung her feet down to the floor and sat up straight. "Listen, I want to run something by you."

I groaned, silently of course. I knew by now that the CO used that phrase when she was about to suggest something that she thought was stupid, that she knew we were going to *know* was stupid, but that some politician somewhere had come up with in order to win a few extra votes in the upcoming "election."

"Lay it on me, Commander." I sat down in the chair reserved for Minions who had been behaving badly and required a private chat about the error of their ways.

"The Quorum is looking for you to go Out-Wall."

I couldn't help it. My hand dropped to my knife and I half came out of the chair, snarling. To her credit, the CO didn't even blink.

"Tell that simpering group of political hacks they can..." I couldn't think of any suggestion that would be horrible enough. Even the long string of profanity, normally ready, twisted and died in my throat. Nicky would have been disappointed.

"It's been three months since the last mass wave," the CO continued. "And that was only the second in six months."

I knew the stats as well as she did. My crew and I faced them every night.

"It's not like all the biodapts got bored and went away." My tone hovered right on the edge of insubordination. "There's real monsters out there, and when they get lucky, we lose real people. My people. Your people."

"Everyone in this compound appreciates their sacrifice." There was a conciliatory tone to the CO's statement. It served as a soft reminder that, like everyone around here who owed their position to the popular vote, she was as much politician as sheriff 'round these parts. As the Protectorate Commandant, she oversaw not just those Protectors who, like us, manned the walls, but also the force of peacekeepers who patrolled inside the In-Wall. She had a lot of lines to toe, and balls to juggle while she stepped to the dance.

Still, not my problem. Dumb orders from politicians—that was her lane. Killing things so that said politicians could stand in front of crowds and boast about how safe they were keeping everyone in the compound—that was my lane. "So why are they asking for my squad to head Out-Wall and get the rest of us killed?"

"It's not just your squad."

I stood up out of my chair, hand resting blatantly on my knife. "Then why am I the only one here right now?"

"Back off, Sera, before I see you and your squad up in front of a tribunal."

The small office left me no place to back off to. I settled for retreating to the farthest wall and leaned my back up against it, arms crossed. A couple of annoying tendrils of hair were escaping my bun, and I glared as I tucked them over my ear.

"You remember last week's session?" The CO relaxed again, leaning back and propping her feet up.

The sudden realization must have showed on my face. I suck at playing cards.

"Glad to see the lightbulb's finally going off." She and I were some of the few left who would still understand that figure of speech.

"This has to do with the shortages?"

"You didn't hear me say this," she replied, "but we crossed over from self-sufficient a while ago and we're heading into heavy rationing. The civilians are already feeling the crunch, and they're starting to talk about cutting into Protector rations."

"So why are you sending the Minions?"

"Because I know you already take risks." The CO nodded at the stack of paperwork under her boots. "That right there is a stack of bullshit shining me on about how your squad never, ever leaves the wall and never, ever takes off on unsanctioned hunting trips."

"Nobody ever asks if the meat we bring back is unsanctioned." I couldn't bite back the sarcastic retort.

The CO shrugged and stood. 'Sergeant Wachhoff, you got two choices, and at this point I don't give a crap which one you pick. You take this mission, and you and your Minions finally get to prove you're the biggest, baddest asses around."

"Or?"

"Or, I arrest you for treason and insubordination, send the rest of your squad for re-training, and some other squad with less experience Out-Wall will take the mission and probably all die gruesome deaths."

That was no choice, and she knew it. She didn't wait around to hear my answer, swinging her feet to the floor and dusting off her uniform before grabbing the stack of reports on my desk and stalking out. Just before the threshold, she paused to glare at me. I'm not a short woman, and I have several inches on her, but she still gave me the perception she was staring down her nose. I waited for her to say something else, but she just shook her head and headed out.

"Minions." My squad had taken on the name as a barb, a play on a dictatorial CO who had treated us as stepping stones in his nascent political career. At first it was a joke, then the joke wore off, and what can I say? That CO didn't make it back from one mission or another. The city certainly didn't mourn the loss of another politician. I'm not even sure how they still exist, except there never seems to be a shortage of people willing to trade small pieces of their humanity for a slightly more comfortable cot and the ability to tell other people what to do.

But anyway, we kept the name. We had kind of gotten used to it and, by now, it would be bad luck to change it.

I had debated waiting until our next stand-to to tell the crew, but that would be taking the coward's way out. Also, facing tough missions and breaking bad news were two of the reasons I earned the right to call myself Sergeant and the keys to my own room in the barracks. That, plus the stacks of paperwork, added up to just about all the perks of my position.

The squad ate dinner—breakfast? Whatever you call the last meal before you hit the rack—in the small cafeteria reserved exclusively for the Protectors. I brought my plate through the line, noticing not for the first time how the food selection had definitely thinned. There were potatoes, and lots of those, but the meat selection was mostly gravy and grudgingly portioned. The only thing vaguely reminiscent of fresh food was the pile of shriveled apples at the end of the line. I filled my canteen at the spigot and looked around for my first team leader.

I found him sitting in an alcove with the other team leaders. Each squad was made of up four teams, and these men and women were responsible for leading teams of three Protectors each. We'd made a habit of eating dinner together, post-mission. Sometimes the team leaders' families or current significant others would join us, but this time, it was just us. They moved their chairs closer together, making room for me at the table.

"So what is it?" Big Mike asked through a mouth full of food. He was a large man, with every ounce on him straight muscle, and it was hard to squeeze in next to him at the table. His close-cropped beard was showing signs of gray in the brownish-red, but a little bit of silver didn't seem to affect his appeal to the ladies and gentlemen who visited his barracks room on a rotating basis. Although, there was one who seemed to be visiting more regularly.

I shook my head, not wanting to go too far down that path of thought, ate a bit of the mashed potatoes and almost gagged. They had been prepared simply by boiling and squishing and were dry as hell. Swigging water from my canteen, I tried not to choke to death in front of my squad.

"We're going to start going Out-Wall." I ran my tongue around my teeth, trying to dislodge the potatoes caked in there. Mixing all the food on my plate together, I successfully avoided eye contact for at least a few seconds. Trying another mouthful of apple, gravy and potato, I finally lifted my head and met four blank stares. "On purpose. Fully sanctioned."

"How far out they want us to go?" My third team leader hadn't been in his position long. A skinny, dark kid, Nass had been transferred from another squad when his entire team had been torn to pieces in a mass attack three months ago.

My words came slowly, carefully. I straddled the line between letting the Minions know that it wasn't my idea to waste their lives, and at the same time taking ownership of the mission. Again, it might not have been my idea, but it was my job. To their credit, there wasn't any of the cranky whining and bullshit you might find in another squad.

"We're going to start with a cloverleaf recon pattern." I drew the pattern on the table with the butt of my knife. "Each team will take a cardinal direction. Tomorrow night we're not going farther than a couple klicks out, same shit we've done before only this time we're actually supposed to be doing it."

"Whadda they got us looking for we ain't already found?" Big Mike, blunt as ever.

"We'll be targeting biodapt nests." Shortly after she'd left my office, the CO had sent a runner with the order from higher, and I'd scanned it for the important parts. I scooped up another mouthful of food. I knew we were rationing, but I dumped it back on my plate. I wasn't hungry. "And locating potential resources for exploitation."

My team leaders weren't dumb, and they read between the lines quicker than I had. They had noticed the decline in the amount and quality of the food before I had—for some of them, three hots and a cot were why they had joined the

Protectors to begin with. And being one of the few squads that had actually ventured Out-Wall, as unsanctioned as our actions had been, it made sense for us to go.

"Sounds like fun, Sarge." My fourth team leader, a tall woman who went by the nickname "Ladyfingers" after losing three of her own digits to a particularly hungry biodapt, grinned. "Can't wait to see the sights."

I eyed my second team leader who hadn't said anything. "Tony? You got anything?"

He shook his head. "You going to eat that?"

I handed him my plate. "Brief your teams, kiss the fam, and be ready to go at stand-to. Everyone draws sixty extra rounds, and I want each of your teams to carry heavy."

Big Mike grunted and saluted with his fork. "Let's do this. Sooner we head out, sooner we get to eating something worth eating."

I didn't feel any better about handing them this soup sandwich, but I knew they would make the best of it. We were the Minions. We took shit and dished it out. And if we made it back in one piece from this mission, it would be a miracle.

Day sleeping has never come naturally to me, but we'd been running the night shift for about a month, and I was almost used to it, just in time to switch back to days in a couple weeks. We slept in what I think used to be a hotel, designed to be cooled with a central air conditioning system. Most of the year we either froze under the sheets or sweated buckets. I pulled the heavy curtain back from the window, hoping to catch a little breeze through the missing glass, and settled into my cot in the barracks, fully expecting to have to chase sleep down and wrestle it into submission.

This morning, though, I fell asleep almost immediately, and as soon as I closed my eyes—I wished I hadn't.

From the darkness and the claustrophobia that closed in, choking and dusty, I knew I was back in the factory. I don't know why my nightmare brain sends me there, but that night, I wandered once again through the labyrinthine building, hearing my guys screaming out, calling for me. I kept coming on bodies, faces—some nothing more than shadows in the dark, some highlighted by the sort of mysterious light one finds in dreams—but as usual, the only people I ever found were the ones I'd lost. They didn't speak, but still told me to keep looking and I did, to find only more of the faces of the dead. Sometimes they had something to say to me. Sometimes they didn't.

Tonight, though, something new stalked the shadows, something beyond detection of the normal five senses. Something followed behind, so close its breath came damp on my heels. The rational voice that somehow survives dreams told me to stop and turn around, but my body wouldn't do it. Instead, I kept moving, faster, into the crowd of accusations of the dead.

The first half of the patrol passed uneventfully, other than a general sense of ambivalent anticipation. Half the thrill of patrolling Out-Wall was the fact that we weren't supposed to do it in the first place. Having been specifically told to do so took away most of the adventure, leaving in its place a mixture of boredom and dread.

Still, Big Mike's team bagged a full-grown deer that didn't exhibit any obvious physical deformities, and even Nass's team came back with an assortment of small, furry creatures. I spent the first part of the patrol with Tony and his team out to the east, while Ladyfingers and her crew ranged up north. We found no sign of any biodapt nests, but then again we really hadn't expected to.

Come midnight, we rendezvoused at the northern gate, handing off the carcasses to the city patrol and grabbing a quick re-fill on water and supplies before heading back out. As long as we weren't ranging much farther out than ten kilometers or so, we would be able to make these stops at home base. Once we started venturing out into the real wilderness, we would have to plan to be on our own. But we had to walk before we could run; that would come later.

I headed out for the second part of the night with Big Mike's team. I planned to keep rotating the teams in different directions every six hours of the twelve-hour shift, to alleviate boredom and to keep us sharp, constantly scouting new territory. Big Mike's plan was to spiral out in a fan pattern until we reached the deep river that ran to the south of the city. We'd seen it on old maps, but had never made it that far ourselves.

Nicky cussed and slapped at his neck. Big Mike reached out and smacked him on the helmet, a reminder to stay quiet. You never knew what was listening out there in the dark.

"Sorry, chief." Nicky's attempt at a whisper sounded like a thunderclap. "Shit ass mosquito."

Big Mike growled, the sound rumbling softly. Nicky took the hint and shut up.

We were moving in close formation through thick undergrowth. Although the moon had almost reached her maximum fullness, the tree canopy periodically cut us off from any illumination. The Minions were used to the darkness, though. Big Mike paused every so often to check his azimuth and kept us on track.

It took us a full three hours to make it through the deep

woods, constantly circling back, taking a knee every so often to check our position and investigate any shadows that could possibly be hiding a nest of biodapts. The team kept an eye in all directions, including above us—you never know when something full of nasty teeth and rabid mech would choose to drop down on you for a midnight snack.

Our first clue that we were coming up on the edge of known territory was the gradual lessening of the darkness before us. At first, it was a simple lightening of the haze surrounding us, but as we continued, we could discern shafts of white slanting through the trees.

Shortly thereafter, the wood line ended in a clearing of waist-high wild grasses. We took cover under the trees for several long moments, letting our eyes adjust, waiting to see what awaited us out in the opening.

"Zzt." The curious buzzing came from Big Mike, who gestured his team up and forward. We stalked, crouching, through the grasses that petered out about fifty meters from the edge of the forest, sloping down to the soft banks of a wide river.

The slow-running water moved black against the gray banks of grasses, its ripples and eddies barely discernible, except where the moon reflected herself back to the sky. She was getting lower against the horizon; dawn wasn't far off. Once she left us, and the sun took her place in the East, I wanted to be safely home and snoring in the barracks. It's harder to hide from monsters when there are no shadows.

It was second nature to take up a prone position at the halt, and the team sank down around us, wide enough to get a 360-degree view of anything sneaking up on us, but within kicking distance if we had to get someone's attention. Big Mike and I lay on our bellies, staring out at the river, muttering as quietly as we could back and forth to each other. The dew from the grasses seeped into the fabric of our uniforms. As Big Mike leaned over to whisper, I caught the hint of tobacco and mint before the night breeze wafted it away, leaving the smells of river mud in its place.

"How far out they expect us to go?"

I shrugged and squinted over the top of my rifle. "No idea." I pitched my voice even more quietly. "Get the feeling they want us to keep going out and out until we get to the point we don't come back."

Big Mike grunted. It's not that I thought the Council wanted us gone or dead. Just that they were willing for us to sacrifice ourselves on the altar of their incompetence.

Some small insect was crawling up my leg, and I was about ready to call it a night. "I think—"

Mike nudged me with his elbow and then pointed his gaze across the river. I followed where he was looking.

I heard them before I saw them. The howl started with a single, lonely voice, tentative at first, then gaining confidence as first one, then another joined in. The sound froze me, there on the ground, sending jolts of adrenaline through my body as I forced myself not to jump up and run. One of the team would let us know if anything encroached on our position, drawn by the howls, but I still felt too exposed.

Even with the moon shining down, it was hard to see across the river to the other bank where, now, the howling was dying down. But one or two of the four-legged creatures had white fur that stood out. I held my breath, waiting for the image to resolve into the weird, irregular forms we'd come to expect.

Off to my side, motion caught my eye. Nicky had raised his rifle, sighting along it at the creatures across the river. I realized it just in time and reached out to kick him in the side. He was mid-trigger pull, but the kick made him flinch and he wasn't that good a shot anyway. The round went so wide, we couldn't see where it impacted. At the sound, the pack across the river alerted, noses in the air, frozen for a half a moment under the moonlight, and then swirled away, slinking through the growing shadows, back into the trees on the other side of the water.

Big Mike pushed himself up on a knee and gave the signal to get up and get moving. Without a word, the team got to their feet and headed back the way we came, finding our own path back through the forest to the Wall, the compound, and safety.

"I don't get it." Nicky was pouting, and it wasn't a good look. "I had the shot and you ruined it. That's shit crap."

"Nicky, shut the fuck up." Big Mike and I looked around the square, but no one was paying attention. The rest of the team had gathered around the table, cleaning weapons again. I didn't think we looked suspicious, but it was our first night Out-Wall, sanctioned, and we'd probably have some interested parties trying to catch some gossip.

"What the hell is he talking about?" Ladyfingers always managed to finish cleaning her weapon before us. I had no idea how she did it, but she gave it one last wipe and closed it up, then sat forward in her chair.

"We saw a whole shit-ass pack of them, and Sarge here wouldn't let me shoot them." Nicky was having trouble disassembling the bolt on his M249. Ladyfingers took it from him and showed him how to get the little pin out that held it together. Each team had one of the larger squad automatic weapons, usually making the new guy carry the heavier weight, and Nicky was no exception. The SAW would be his until someone newer came along, and then he'd be the one showing them the ropes.

"First, they were all the way across the water, and none of them had gills, so there was no reason to waste a round," I said. "Also, you shoot like a squirrel having a seizure, and there's no way you would have hit one, so again, saving rounds."

Nicky bristled, but couldn't think of anything to say, not even an ineffective cuss word.

"And finally, those weren't biodapts."

"What?" Nicky stared. "Of course they were—I saw them."

"Well, if you saw them, it was because you weren't looking where you were supposed to," Big Mike told Nicky with a glare. "So we'll work on that before chow."

Nicky finally shut his mouth and subsided into his chair, furiously wiping carbon off the bolt.

"You sure they weren't, Sarge?" Nass stared. "We haven't seen anything out there except deer that weren't some kind of deformed in years."

"I'm sure." At first, I hadn't been, but the more we'd looked, the more certain I'd become.

"We know what we saw," Big Mike said. "And you all are going to keep this to yourselves until we find out what the Council and every other elected official in this place has planned for these excursions."

"They just want us to hunt more meat," Nicky groused.

Big Mike looked at his watch. "Turn in your weapon and meet me at Nasty Nelly in two minutes."

Nicky stared at Big Mike. "But ... what the crap?"

"If you've got time to be this much of a dumbass, you have time to train," he snarled, and Nicky jumped out of his seat. "Get going."

Nicky took off, and Big Mike shook his head. Nobody

thought we were going out there simply for the chance to get some fresh meat. The Council always had an ulterior motive. At least negotiating the obstacle course would either give Nicky time to think about that, or tire him out until he was too exhausted to say dumb shit.

"Well, Sarge?" Ladyfingers broke the silence, looking from me to Mike and back to me. "What were they?"

"Wolves." And then, with a note of wonder I couldn't keep out of my voice, "True wolves."

———

There's not much to say about what came before. I was just a kid when it happened, too little to understand much, and then there weren't that many people interested in helping us understand. My dad had been someone relatively important in the old world, I guess; in the new, he'd shepherded my brother and I through the worst of it. Not that anyone got off easy. But he'd been in a position to see things going sideways and helped prepare this compound against the things that the other side had engineered against us.

Most of the urban areas away from water dried up and drifted away like blood from a scab. But here, we had water, resources, guns, and people willing to use the latter to protect and take the former. When I was ten years old, and the In-Wall had first gone up, we'd seen our first biodapt. Short for biologically adapted. Some kind of mutant monsters that threw themselves against the walls. Sometimes you could tell what animal they had been based on—dogs, mostly. A couple of bears. Once, even a monkey. And sometimes, they looked almost human under their mods.

The Protectorate had been formed to patrol the area between

the In- and Out-Wall. A typical patrol for our team meant walking a route between the two walls, a long, fertile strip of land where laborers farmed crops by day and we guarded shadows by night, protected by the stationary towers on either wall. My team had been sneaking out on short patrols Out-Wall the past year and a half. The CO had been right—attacks had been declining in frequency, and we had wanted to see what was out there, not for any other reason than that Out-Wall was there for us to explore.

But now, the food was dwindling, and the politicians were tightening their belts, and it was time for us to be sent out onto those paths. I wondered what my dad would think about that. Or my brother, killed three years ago in a particularly vicious attack when three biodapts made it through the Out-Wall while his team was on patrol.

Neither he nor I had ever had much interest in elected office, but more than once I had found myself wondering if we had been mistaken not to follow in Dad's footsteps. If we could have done something other than patrol until the biodapts threw themselves at the Walls. If we could have proven that the Protectorate, which wore the uniforms Dad had worn and owed everything to his training, could have been more than just the reactionary force at the whim of the politicians that we turned out to be. And if it was too late, now, to change any of that.

Sleep came easy that morning, but it didn't bring much rest. I found myself back in the twisting maze of corridors and dead ends. This time, I was plagued by the dream notion that there was a door, an exit, just to the right of the area we were running through.

We? Wait. No, my team had been at my heels, but as I turned, I was alone.

No. Not alone. As I walked down the corridor, the wood floor and white walls darkened, then vanished, and became a path through an old forest. In the gloom, the trees arched overhead, and occasionally, through the screen of birch and pine on either side, I caught glimpses of things moving deep within. The damp smell of dirt and loam and moisture hanging rich in the air flowed around me. Behind me, unseen but, with the strange sense one gets in dreams, very definitely there, padded the thick, muted steps of a wolf. This was a big one, bigger than the ones we'd seen at the river.

My blood ran cold, and I tried to start running, but my dream body refused to obey, and I stumbled forward in a walk that I desperately wished were a run. Or even a slow jog. The biodapt wolf behind me—again, there was no certainty except what the dream could tell me—kept pace.

A thick, blueish fog lit the path before me, and a murder of crows called as they burst from cover, whirled overhead, and disappeared. In the clearing ahead, a silhouette greeted me. I realized, this was what I had been following, and although I hadn't seen it before, I somehow accepted it had been there to guide my panicked steps through the maze. Another wolf, a real wolf. The huge gray animal with the white markings faced me and snarled, and the presence at my back drifted to smoke.

She caught my eye, held my gaze, then faded away into the light.

———

The day was so hot and humid we were all dripping before we left the Out-Wall. The tall, green walls of the forest surrounding us made it worse, concentrating the sun and beaming its rays down on us, coaxing the moisture from the dirt and the leaves. It had rained in the night, and as we walked, we brushed against the leftover crops. By the time we made it a klick out, we were thoroughly drenched.

Our night shift had ended, and we were back on day patrol. This time, with less cover and more activity from the biodapts during the hours of sunlight, the Council had seen fit to approve two squads to patrol.

Ladyfingers held up a hand, calling a halt, just as I walked through a particularly wet and sticky cobweb. I flailed at my face and walked straight into a low-hanging branch that sent droplets down my neck and back.

I cussed silently to myself, then heard what she had called the halt for.

Gunfire.

The shots came from the northwest, away from the gate. As the team took up a protective position around us, I knelt near Ladyfingers so we could talk without anything nearby overhearing.

"One team, maybe two engaging." Ladyfingers nodded in the opposite direction. "Big Mike and Nass are patrolling south, we're closest."

I knew what she was saying. If anyone was going to respond, it would have to be us. Rules of engagement called for us to come to the aid of the other squad; but depending on the size of the nest they'd run into, survival would possibly—probably—mean booking it in the opposite direction, back to the gate.

More shots. They weren't too far away, but not so close that we couldn't make a tactical withdrawal. There was a short moment of silence, and then another flurry of gunfire, this time a long series of rounds that went on and on, one set of weapons engaging, then another. Disciplined shooting. But with a rapid-fire cadence to it.

"Let's go." I nodded in the direction of the sound of the fire. They were still in the fight. "If the firing stops, we stop."

Ladyfingers nodded, understanding, then signaled for her team to get moving. We spread out, taking advantage of the lack of undergrowth to move in a loose "V" shape. Coming up on another unit when they were currently engaging the biodapts could be tricky; it's easy to mistake even a fellow Protector for an enraged half-monkey or deformed raccoon when the adrenaline is pounding through your body and your finger's on the trigger.

The firefight kept up, growing in intensity as we stalked through the woods. We moved quickly, worrying less than usual about making a sound. All the noise was coming from ahead of us. Sweating, slipping in the damp mud and leaves, we finally reached the edge of where the crack and thunder of the weapons hurt the eardrums.

Halfway up a washout, a pack of chittering, slavering creatures leapt and bounded, trying to reach what was left of a team of Protectors. The cliffside surrounding the washout on three sides was steep enough that the furred biodapts were having trouble reaching the Protectors, but not so steep that they wouldn't eventually succeed. Two of the team had reached the top. One, a woman bleeding profusely from the scalp, tried to help a fellow teammate up the loose, sandy hill, while the other, a man whose dark skin was slashed with a number of deep, red cuts, laid down covering fire.

At the bottom of the hill, almost completely covered by the swarming pack, I caught a glimpse of bloody canvas, a scrap of leather, the end of a barrel on a tripod. A thick, furred mass scurried and trampled in waves, feeding on the remains of the two Protectors who hadn't made it to safety.

There was no time to find the best position for an attack. The terrain around the washout would protect us for a short amount of time. We had the high ground, flanking the defending team and the biodapts, and we'd have to make it work. Taking up prone positions at the edge of the wood, we began firing down at the biodapts.

The shots barely got their attention. As one would fall, another would take its place.

"Holy shit, Sarge!" Ladyfingers yelled, firing again into the pack. "They're healing faster than we can kill them."

"They're not healing," I yelled back, then paused, sighting and shooting two more. They jerked, flipped, and disappeared under their fellows. "There's just so many of them."

Finally, our shots caught their attention. One by one, the creatures paused to look up at us. They were quadrupeds, with thick fur and sharp teeth, and claws that curved around with wicked barbs at the end. They looked almost like beavers or groundhogs or raccoons, but their faces had been morphed into nightmares, no longer the dumb, passive gazes of herbivoral mammals. Instead, reflected up at us, from what seemed like a thousand pairs of eyes, came the craving, murderous drive to kill and eat that drove the biodapts.

"Christ, Sarge, you think they'll—"

I knew what Ladyfingers was going to say and cursed her for putting the words into the universe, because as soon as she said it, the biodapts abandoned their attempts to get at us by scaling the cliff. Instead, the pack began sniffing around, shuffling around the terrain, flowing up the sides, getting closer to finding where the terrain sloped down, providing them access to climb the ridge and come after us.

"Shit, shit, shit!"

I don't know who said it, but panic reverberated their words throughout the team.

"Shift fire, shift fire, you bastards!" Ladyfingers screamed, and the team turned as one to face the new, incoming threat. "Take cover! Shoot the little furry assholes!"

"Fuck 'em all!" The Minions erupted in laughter, and I joined them, even as panic and fear lent my words a hard, ragged edge.

And then things went from bad to worse. The biodapts found the path and the swarm regained its footing, tumbling and growling and glistening with blood and saliva.

If I'd had any doubts about their intelligence, they were now dispelled. The biodapts moved as if controlled by one mind, flowing up the slope towards us, darting from tree to tree, maintaining cover.

"Shit." Ladyfingers fired, but the round missed its target, pinging off the rock the creature crouched behind. She fired again, too fast, and the lead biodapt came within a few yards before my bullet dropped it, blood trickling from its head.

We fired and fired again. We'd rehearsed this over and over, two members of the team shooting while the other two reloaded, the SAW punctuating our efforts with its rapid fire. But we'd never faced a wave like this before, and even with the rapid machine-gun fire of the automatic weapons, the leading edge of the pack was getting closer.

My ears were already deafened by the wave of shooting. We fired and fell back, fired and fell back, but the biodapts leapt towards us and kept coming. They were close enough that I could see their snarls, but all I could hear was a high-pitched ringing and the dull thud of weapons fire.

The largest biodapts finally made it to our line, darting around the trees and flanking us against the cliffside. We were at the top of the draw, forming a protective semicircle around the wounded members of the other squad, firing desperately.

My bolt clicked to the rear. I was empty. Reaching for another magazine, I came up short.

"Fuck." Trying not to panic, I patted down every single pouch and pocket I had, but in the maelstrom, I had fired until empty like a rookie dumbass. "Shit."

Ladyfingers tossed me a magazine and kept firing.

A trio of biodapts rushed the first of us, a kid whose real name I couldn't remember but who everyone called Smokes. He was empty, but kept pulling at the trigger, screaming as the creatures swarmed over him. A spray of bright red, and his scream cut off.

Time slowed.

I turned, firing, moving without thinking, without being consciously aware of what I was doing. Something burned down my left leg. Something punctured the skin in my lower back, tearing flesh until I grabbed it, pulling it from me, stomping as the blood flowed from the wound. The swarm was all around us now. I pulled my knife and said a brief prayer to a Goddess I'd stopped believing in, and hacked and slashed and shot long after the blade went slick in my hand.

The unearthly howl penetrated even the ringing in my ears. The biodapts froze as one, the swarm momentarily still. By now, their ranks had been decimated, but a good twenty or thirty of the little bastards were still on us.

Taking advantage of the distraction, I slashed and kicked at the biodapt at my feet, almost losing my knife in its thick fur.

The howling came again, and this time the first voice was joined by a feral chorus. The sound reverberated through the woods. The firing had stopped; we had all run out of rounds.

I turned, looking for Ladyfingers, or for any member of the squad for that matter. All I found around me was a charnel ground of fur and mud and blood and bone.

The biodapts closest to me recovered, snarling. They turned as one, and I gripped my knife, ready to go down under their teeth, ready to fight until they stripped my flesh and left my bones to rot.

A huge gray blur knocked the wind from me, pushing me to the ground as it ran past and grabbed the biodapt by the throat. With a quick shake, the biodapt's neck broke, and the monstrous gray creature was on to the next.

I sat in disbelief, knife still clenched in my hand, dripping blood, coated in it. The first gray wolf was joined by a wave of ten more, massive beasts with thick fur that caught the sunlight as it dappled through the trees, turning red at the tips in the slaughter. They bit and howled and snarled, and by the time I thought to bring up my knife to defend against them, they had laid waste to the entire pack of biodapts.

A groan at my side distracted me. Ladyfingers was half-sitting, half-laying, propped up against the body of one of the Protectors we'd come to support. The man with the deep scores on his body was beyond aid, limbs flopping uselessly. Ladyfingers coughed and groaned again; most of what should have been inside her torso lay strewn across the leaves. A biodapt that had been feasting on her guts had been tossed to the side by the wolves' onslaught.

That's what they were. Wolves. True wolves. As the pack finished their slaughter, sniffing here and there to make sure that no biodapt stirred further, the biggest wolf alerted. Tail and ears up, she sniffed the air. Her gaze slid over to me, and I gripped the knife tighter.

She walked to me, slowly, as if giving me time to decide what to do. There was no fear in her. As she came closer, I recognized her. We had seen her pack at the river. She had been the lead wolf there, the white ears and tail amid the otherwise gray fur setting her apart.

"Damn, Sarge, she's beautiful." Ladyfingers reached out to the wolf, who bowed her head. Then, with a rasping gargle, my Protector dropped her arm. I waited to hear her next breath, but it never came.

I tried to get to my feet and fell to one knee. The wolves didn't react, just watched me. I breathed slowly, feeling every ache and cut and slash, now that the fight was over. My hands shook, and I almost dropped the knife.

Get a grip. Pulling myself together, I forced myself to my feet. The cut on my leg was still bleeding, but it wouldn't kill me before I got back to the Wall.

That is, if the wolves would let me pass.

Figuring they would either kill me or let me by, but there wasn't much I could do about it either way, I started moving. Stumbling at first, I gathered up the identification tags from each of the fallen, tucking them safely in one of my empty magazine pouches. I slipped Ladyfingers's wedding ring from her left hand and clipped that to one of the carabiners on my kit to give to her wife if I made it back to the compound.

Groaning, I slung every rifle I could recover over my back, hefting two or three before I decided that was enough. I picked up the M249, which still had a few more rounds in the belt. The previous gunner's fingers slid to the ground one by one. The rest of the previous gunner was nowhere to be seen.

A gentle breeze wafted through the trees, drying the sweat and gore on my arms and the back of my neck. The ringing had faded somewhat, but I still couldn't hear much over the dull roar that washed over my eardrums. I took a deep breath, and the air tasted of blood and dirt.

Limping but still making good time, I slogged back to the

main gate. The sun wasn't quite setting; it was barely past mid-afternoon. Still, the woods around me were quiet, the wind picking up, preparing for the night. Insects swarmed and landed, and I slapped at them without much effect.

I don't recall most of the hike back; half the time I was shaking like a leaf, the straps of the rifles digging into my shoulder, struggling to put one foot in front of the other. The other half ... I don't remember well. At one point, I forgot about the attack and convinced myself that I was heading to my squad's position. The conviction that they were being attacked and I had to go find them settled in my brain, and I turned and started walking off in another direction entirely, fixated on the idea that I could save them.

A friendly growl stopped me in my tracks and brought me back to myself. The big female wolf with the white markings stood a few meters away. With the late afternoon sunlight filtering through the trees, I hadn't seen her. She yipped, and the soft noise brought me back to myself. I raised my hand to my kit and touched Ladyfingers's wedding ring.

I looked around for the rest of her pack. I couldn't see them—not quite, but I knew they were there. The idea that they were shepherding me back to the gate, unseen yet shadowing my steps, gave me a fresh burst of energy, and I got back on my way, heading back to the gate and the safety of the compound.

———

I woke up and was still in pain. Meds were at a premium, especially painkillers, and since the worst was over, the docs were being stingy. The cut on my leg had required stitches, and they had done some patching up on my back as well. The CO had given me a couple days to rest and recuperate, and I was spending most of it in my room.

The knock on the door meant that someone wanted me for something, and so I ignored it.

They knocked again.

"Sarge, I know you're in there. Open the fucking door."

I groaned. Of course Big Mike was going to come looking for answers. When I finally got up and opened the door, I was even less surprised to see the other team leaders standing there.

"All right, let me get my boots on."

Big Mike, Nass, and Tony met me out behind Nasty Nelly. The rest of the Minions—what was left of us—gathered around. I didn't want a big audience, and anyone who saw us out there would hopefully not look too close at a squad doing some extra training on the obstacle course. Eventually, I'd get the CO a full report, but I owed it to the Minions to tell them what had happened first. I'd already stopped by Ladyfingers's place to give her wife the ring I'd brought back.

I started with hearing the sounds of firing in the woods, not flinching or backing down as I related my decision to take Ladyfingers's team. To lead them into the ambush.

My voice thickened, and I stumbled over my words, trying to keep my own misery from overwhelming what I had to tell them. I paused, and Big Mike met my gaze. He didn't try to pat my shoulder or comfort me, just nodded and grunted. That helped me keep going, and I choked out the rest of the story.

When I was done, the team leaders exchanged glances, but no one wanted to be the first to say something.

"Shitting hell, Sarge." Nicky shook his head.

"Shut up, Nicky." Big Mike cuffed him, but there wasn't any force behind it. "Those wolves walked you all the way back to the compound?"

I shrugged. It was the truth, and they could take it or leave it, but I wasn't the sort to lie to my squad.

"Huh." Mike scratched his chin where he was working on a two-day five o'clock shadow.

"I've seen them." Nass shuddered. "When my squad got tore up."

"That attack a few months back?" Tony asked.

"Yeah." Nass's dark eyes were almost unreadable as he met my gaze. He had been the sole survivor, and hadn't had much to say about the attack, even in the official reports. "That one."

There was a beat, and then I prompted him with: "What happened?"

"We were manning the southeast Out-Wall." Nass's voice was dry, remote. "Things started climbing the wall. We fought them, and they kept coming. Then ... they stopped coming."

"I remember that report," Big Mike said. "They said it was big lizard-looking things."

Nass nodded. "Climbed right up the walls. We kept shooting, and they swarmed over us. Backup squad got the ones that got past us, but the only reason they stopped coming..." He shrugged. "I was the only one left, and I didn't even believe it, so I didn't say anything."

"You saw them, too." I thought back to the huge wolf who had led her pack, wiped out the creatures, and then kept me on the path back to the gate.

Nass hesitated, then nodded.

"What are we going to do?" Big Mike leaned back and folded his arms.

That was a good question, and I didn't have a ready

answer, but I did have a dozen faces staring at me, waiting for me to make a decision.

"First thing we're gonna do is keep our mouths shut," I said. "I still owe the CO a debrief; I'll take care of that." I looked around at each of the Minions, gathering them into the circle of confidence. "Mike, Tony, Nass—I want you to reach out, *quietly*, to some of the other teams, see if they've seen anything strange. Anything like..." I thought for a moment. "Anything strange. Tell them—don't tell them not to fire if they get attacked, but don't go shooting at something that's not snarling at you, got it?"

They nodded, understanding. If the pack was out there, acting somehow like great, big guard dogs, we didn't want anyone shooting at them. On the other hand, it was better to get more clarity on what the hell they even were before bringing it up the chain. All our higher command were politicians, and one thing you could always trust elected officials to do, was fuck everything up.

Nothing ached and the lacerations on my leg had disappeared. That's how I knew it was a dream. That and the hot breath on my naked heels. Running. I was running, and I was barefoot—no, I was completely bare, running outside. It was night, but I could still see. I stopped to catch my breath, slowing down as everything came at me in shades of green and gray, and my breath burned in my lungs as I panted in the cold air.

And then I was walking as fast as I could, only this time I was back in the factory and my feet slapped through puddles on the concrete floor. I didn't dare look behind me. If I turned, they would catch up, the snarling, furred creatures with the faces of insanity.

My fists clenched and I pumped my arms, but I couldn't seem to go faster; I barely broke into a jog. My body refused to move, slowing.

Slaver dripped onto my calves and heels. As if coming out of deep water, I found myself able to run again. I sprinted past dead Protectors. Their fingertips brushed me, but didn't grasp or cling. I powered through, not stopping even when the last Protector stood to face me. Ladyfingers—her guts spilling from her open abdomen, her arm raised and pointed toward—

An open door. Right in front of me. A giant rectangle through which bright sunlight spilled. And, silhouetted in the middle, a giant gray wolf.

I didn't slow. As I ran for the door, the wolf bunched her muscles under her and leapt.

She came straight for me, until it seemed we must collide, her legs outstretched, teeth bared, muzzle just barely touching my chest.

And then we were gone, beyond the path in the forest, beyond the long, narrow corridors of the factory, out into a place that was many places at once as the wolf and I ran along an endless road of light.

The staff runner was a skinny kid who I swore couldn't have been more than sixteen? Seventeen? It had to be a sign of getting older that all the new recruits looked like kids. She jolted to a stop at the door to my squad's office and panted until she caught her breath.

"CO needs to see you, Sergeant." She straightened and

started to salute, then remembered that she didn't need to and sort of let her hand flop. It reminded me disconcertingly of Ladyfingers's last gesture.

"Tell her I'm on my way to her office." I sighed, not unhappy for an interruption in the paperwork, but not really looking forward to what I knew would be orders Out-Wall. We'd had a nice week's reprieve; looked like it was at an end.

"Sorry, Sergeant, she needs you to meet her at Council HQ." The runner bobbed nervously. "She said she'll meet you there and to double time."

"Roger, Private, I'm on my way."

The kid stood there for a few seconds.

"Anything else?"

She blinked. "I'm supposed to take you there."

With great effort, I refrained from rolling my eyes or saying out loud what I thought of the CO's order. Grabbing my hat, I set my pen down and stood up, making a big deal of stretching, especially my left leg, which was still not fully healed, then limped after her.

We made a brief stop at the barracks. Getting called to HQ was never a good sign, and I wanted to let Big Mike know what was going on. Besides, I was pretty sure I knew what they wanted to see me for.

I knocked and waited outside long enough to prevent walking in on embarrassing situation. For as long as he'd been with the squad, Big Mike's barracks door had been a constantly revolving rotation of men and women. For the last few months, though, he'd been seeing one guy, Kenny, who worked in the armory. Either way I wanted Big Mike's private life to stay private, and so I stood outside the door with the runner who shifted nervously from foot to foot while we waited.

Mike opened the door. "Sarge. They sending us back out?"

In the background, his boyfriend caught sight of me and sighed and pulled his shirt on.

"Yeah, I'm being summoned." I nodded at the runner. "Big-wigs have something important for us. Probably want us to go recover weapons and brass."

I didn't want to take my entire squad—what was left of it—back to the killing ground to pick up some rifles and brass, but the weapons were expensive and impossible to replace. Plus the brass could be melted down and used again, so there really was no way to get out of it.

"Let's get ready and prep the squad," I told Mike. "Grab extra rounds and be green to go when I get back. Sooner we get this over and get everyone back In-Wall, the better."

"Roger, Sarge." Mike nodded and closed the door. We headed out of there quickly. I didn't want to hear him getting busy saying goodbye to Kenny.

The Council headquarters building was about a kilometer and a half down the road, guaranteeing that we would walk in sweaty and dripping. Luckily, there was a water point set up outside the front gate, and after the runner showed our pass to the gate guard, we were able to wash up.

The HQ building served as the central gathering place when the compound needed to come together; that, however, was rarer and rarer. Usually, the people working in the building would be the representatives of the various districts and their staffs, the Protectorate Commandant, and the heads of the various departments—sanitation, agriculture, education. The building itself was actually a collection of buildings and offices. The main gathering area had once been a church, but now, with the proliferation of Gods and Goddesses, worshipping them had become a source of fracture, not unity, and their sacred spaces had been relegated to areas that couldn't be put to any better use. As for me, I grew up worshipping the Queen of Battle, although as I got older, I suspected that my father had set her up as an inside joke, and I'd fallen away from making the offerings at her shrine in the Protectorate compound.

Walking into the hall, I was struck by a sudden memory of walking in with Dad, tagging along on some business or other. For all of his talk of merit and democracy, my brother and I had figured out early on that he was grooming us to follow him in the path of command. It was evident in his pride when we joined the Protectors. He'd died a year before my brother got killed, still under the assumption that we had joined the force as the first step to a political career. Only my brother had ever, briefly, considered that plan; I'd always thought we did more good actually protecting the people who lived in the little civilization we'd carved out of the apocalypse.

"You took your time, Sergeant." The CO looked more pissed off than usual. I decided to do what I normally did when she was really mad at me—kept my mouth shut and waited. She looked me up and down, frowned, and waved the runner away. "Come on, they're waiting for us."

I'd never been up in front of a full tribunal, but I'd sat in the galley when my father presided over a few. Still, that distant memory did nothing to prepare me for the weight of several dozen faces turning our way as we walked in the door. The CO led the way, me dragging my steps behind her, to a table set up in the center of the room.

"What the hell is going on?" I hissed under my breath.

The CO ignored me and waited for the two men and one woman sitting at the front of the room to proceed.

"Commander Collins, Sergeant Wachhoff, you may sit." I recognized the woman, Mayor Alice Tsao. I'd voted for her in the last election, mostly out of laziness. She was a supporter of the Protectors and not egregiously bad at the rest of her job. She led the Council, with the other two members drawn from the district representatives, rotating in six-month shifts. Something was going on here, something more than being sent out to retrieve a half dozen rifles and some brass.

We sat, my legs and knees aching with the effort, my back itchy with the crowd sitting behind us.

The Mayor nodded at the uniformed man standing to the side, a member of the city patrol assigned to peacekeeping duty. He ducked out and returned shortly with a familiar face. What the hell was Nicky doing here?

The Protector led him to another table, a short distance from ours. He sat, very obviously not looking over at us, avoiding my stare.

"Private Nicholas Smith, as a reminder, you are still under oath," Tsao said. "You may state here your testimony in the presence of witnesses."

Nicky gave me a quick glance. *I'm sorry.* He mouthed the words, but I just kept staring back at him.

"Private?" the Mayor prompted.

"Yes, Mayor, sorry, Mayor." Nicky stammered a bit, then kept going. "We found—like I said—the Sergeant found the wolves. I mean, the wolves that she encountered when Lady—Corporal Marshall's team came under attack."

"These wolves, were they biologically adapted mutants?" The question came from one of the district reps I didn't know.

"Um ... the Sergeant said no." Under the table, Nicky's leg was bouncing up and down. "She said they were true wolves."

"And they followed her back to the gate?" Tsao prodded.

"Yes, ma'am—Mayor. Yes, Mayor." Nicky's voice trembled, like he was about to cry. He hadn't tried to throw in a single cuss word.

"Thank you, Private," Tsao said. "You are dismissed."

Nicky threw one last, wild look at us, then scrambled out of his chair and headed out of the hall as fast as he could walk without breaking into a jog.

"Sergeant Wachhoff, you disagree with your squad member's assessment?" Tsao's voice was dry.

"Sera..." the CO hissed. "Watch it."

"What assessment?" I asked. "All I heard was a bunch of bullshit from someone who wasn't even there."

My CO stayed sitting, ramrod straight, smile plastered on her face.

"Indeed," Mayor Tsao answered. "Private Smith's testimony was in fact the only debrief we've received from the incident."

The CO reached out and put her hand on my arm. I shook it off, my eyesight turning red at the edges.

"The incident?" I laughed out loud. "You mean the incident where this Council sent two squads Out-Wall because they don't know how to manage resources, and two teams got ripped to pieces by a swarm of fucking biodapts? You mean that incident?"

"Sera, *sit down.*"

I hadn't realized I'd stood up until the CO whisper-shouted at me. Shaking my head, I swallowed back the memory of the taste of blood in my mouth, of the smell of Ladyfingers's viscera as she died.

"What details are you missing?" I asked. "How much blood is still staining my boots, or the uniform I was wearing? The fact that some of my squad, all that's left of them are bones and dirt? Fuck. If you want us to go back out there and get the weapons, we're ready to go. Just don't—what?" The CO was shaking her head at me.

"We do have a mission for your squad," Mayor Tsao said mildly. "These reports of wolves Out-Wall are concerning. The Council has discussed the potential for attacks and resource competition. Given your squad's previous encounters, we've directed your CO to assign you this mission."

I'm not the most rational person when I *haven't* had a week straight of nightmares, and it took a second for the Mayor's words to sink in. When they did, I ignored my CO's frantic pulling at my sleeve.

"No fucking way."

She gave up and slumped over, face in hands.

"I'm here and alive today because of that pack of wolves." I pitched my voice loud enough to carry throughout the room. "I'd be meat for the biodapts if they hadn't shown up. If that means they want to bring down a deer or two Out-Wall, I'd not only let them, I'd shoot it for them."

I turned and looked around the room, gauging reactions. The Council looked pissed off, my CO looked defeated, and the rest of the crowd was talking and murmuring, but I couldn't catch what they were saying, or what way the mood was shifting. At the back of the room, I caught sight of Big Mike, in uniform, flanked by Nass and Tony. He caught my eye, threw me a question. I shook my head. This was my business to deal with, and I didn't want them to get caught up in it. He subsided, but stayed watchful.

"Sergeant Wachhoff, we have afforded—" The Mayor realized no one was listening, least of all me, and picked up her little gavel, banging it on the desk. The room stilled. "Sergeant Wachoff, in respect to your father and brother, we have cut you a lot of slack. Your CO's have each submitted reports of your insubordination, lack of military bearing, and failure to respect authority."

"And I use fucking cuss words, too, don't forget that," I said. "Most of the time when my Minions and I are keeping your fat asses safe behind Walls, or providing you the meat you forget to ration out to the rest of the citizens." The Mayor started pounding her gavel again, but I was done pretending I gave a shit. "You want to respect my father? Then fucking respect what he built. You want us to protect the Walls? Then you can start by not hunting the first thing Out-Wall that acted like an ally instead of trying to eat us."

"Are you saying that the wolves are allies?" The Mayor scoffed, shaking her head. "Sera Wachhoff, it is the decision of this tribunal that you be stripped of your rank and special privileges as Protector..."

"Fuck you, too."

"...and that you be placed under arrest, until such time as the Council decides your fate. Peacekeeper?"

The city patrolman approached me, hesitant, a pair of handcuffs dangling from his left hand. "Sergeant?"

I turned to face the Council again. "My fate is none of your business." By the time I'd made that lofty pronouncement, the patrolman was in reach. He was expecting me to follow the Council's direction, but I was done taking their orders, and instead balled up my fist and throat-punched him.

He went down choking, and I followed up with a knee to the torso that left him gasping in the fetal position.

The crowd erupted, noise and shouts. Hoping that my team leaders were getting the hell out of there and not doing something stupid, I headed for the side door that we'd come in. Unfortunately for me, an entire squad of Protectors chose that moment to make their entrance, likely primed by the CO to intervene in case of chaos, and I made it about two meters before I was surrounded and tackled to the ground, someone's knee in my back ripping out my stitches, a nightstick at my throat cutting off my air.

The last thought I had was pretty much a string of cuss words, and then something hit the back of my head and turned off the lights.

I wasn't expecting much of a trial, and that's about what I got. A night in one of the cells, and then, as the sun broke over the Wall, a bag over my head and frog-marched to the southeast Out-Wall gate.

Once at the gate, the Protectors guarding me took off the cuffs and removed the bag, leaving me blinking in the early morning sunlight. In addition to the three who had walked me to the gate, the Mayor and my CO—ex-CO now, I guess—had come to deliver the Council's decision.

We were by the gate. I already knew what that decision had been. At least my CO had the grace to look slightly embarrassed as she handed me my knife and a rucksack with a couple of days of rations, a flint and steel, and a change of clothes.

"Sera Wachhoff, formerly Sergeant, your status as citizen under this Council is formally revoked," Mayor Tsao said as I settled the pack on my back and adjusted the straps. "You are hereby exiled from this compound. If you are ever found within ten kilometers of Out-Wall, you will be shot on sight." She shook her head, making a little *tsk-tsk* sound. "What would your father say if he were here?"

"He would tell you to get fucked."

There wasn't really anything to say after that, and no one was in the mood to hang around the Out-Wall gate any longer than they had to. The Protectors opened the door as the assigned gate guards kept watch. They kicked me out, locked it behind me, and that was that.

The bolt sliding home behind me, and the soft murmur of the guards' conversation at the top of the wall faded away. As I walked, the sounds of the forest in summer rose up around me—insects, birds, small creatures rustling. I kept an ear out for anything larger, although I preferred not to think about what I was going to do with my knife against a swarm of biodapts.

For a brief moment, I considered heading back to the scene of the ambush to grab a weapon, but there would be no rounds, and in any case, I wanted to put as much distance between me and the Walls as possible before night fell.

On my own, without a patrol pattern to follow, I made pretty good time. We'd heard rumors of other settlements to the south, along what used to be the Eastern seaboard of the old United States, and I figured I'd head that way for as long as I could, see what I could find.

A twig snapped. I pivoted to face the noise, knife in hand, and waited, the walls of the forest pressing in against the path, pulse pounding in my head.

Big Mike was the first to step out where I could see him. Kenny was next to him, which explained why the rest of the squad was well-armed as the Minions emerged from the woods.

"Sergeant," Big Mike said in greeting. He handed me a rifle and tactical vest. When I took the vest, the weight of loaded magazines gave it an extra heft.

I dropped my pack to put the vest on, then picked it up and settled it back on my shoulders. "You're a bunch of dumbasses, you know that, right?"

Mike shrugged. "Just not interested in following someone else's orders."

I noticed that Nicky wasn't with them. I hoped he was all right. He was a little shit, but he'd been new, and I was intimately familiar with the kind of pressure the Council could bring to bear on someone when they wanted something.

"Where we heading?" Nass spoke up.

"Figured I—we'd—go south," I answered. "See if there's anything to those rumors about settlements down near the coast."

The three team leaders exchanged glances, nodded. Taking direction from the sun, Nass led his team out first. As if we were out on just another patrol, Big Mike's team fell into place, then me, then Tony bringing up the rear.

We moved silently through the rising heat, ears up, eyes out, heads on a swivel, ready for anything.

And, as we made our way south to the questionable promise of human contact, I caught fleeting glimpses of the shadows that paced our steps, and heard whispers of the soft, almost imperceptible sound of stalking paws against the leaves that littered the floor. We were exiles, but we weren't lost.

And we weren't alone.

THE END

ACKNOWLEDGMENTS

No writer is an island, and I am no exception. I've been very lucky to have the support of my spouse as I've taken those first steps in the long, strange trip that is the life of a writer. I could not do this without his love and encouragement, and so thank you, Rob. I am also grateful for the support of my family, especially my mom, who always buys a copy of my books, even when I send her the link to a free download. Love you, Ma.

A number of these stories first found life in a workshop, and I want to acknowledge the fellow writers of the Round Rock Writers' Guild in Round Rock, Texas, as well as the Fayetteville Writers Helping Writers group. An excellent writing group is invaluable, and I couldn't be where I am today without these two in particular.

Thanks as well to Lynne Hansen, whose 31 Days of Art Challenge in 2020 spurred me to get back to the drawing board—or at least the laptop—and get the words churning again. A number of the stories in these pages found life because of that mad dash of a challenge, and I am very grateful.

There are two stories in this collection which are

appearing in public for the first time. I was lucky enough to have fellow writers who were willing to read and send me critiques on "Side Roads" and "And Out Come the Wolves." Thank you especially to DL Wainright, Darin Kennedy, Jen Mierisch, Voss Foster, and Jennifer Nestojko. I owe you big time.

Let me not forget, a shout out to John Hartness, without whose story-naming advice "And Out Come the Wolves" would still be called "Wolf Hunter Story."

And last, but certainly not least, thank you, Reader. I hope the journey was not too arduous, and that you enjoyed these works enough to stick around for what comes next!

ABOUT THE AUTHOR

As a military journalist, Rachel A. Brune wrote and photographed the Army and its soldiers for five years. When she moved on, she didn't quit writing stories with soldiers in them, just added werewolves, sorcerers, a couple evil mad scientists, and a Fae or two. Now a full-time author and writing coach living in North Carolina, Rachel enjoys poking around former military installations and listening for the ghosts of old soldiers ... or writing them into her latest short story. In addition to writing, she is the founder and chief editor of Crone Girls Press, an indie horror micro press dedicated to publishing the dark side of speculative fiction. She lives with her spouse, two daughters, one reticent cat, and two flatulent rescue dogs.

Stay up-to-date with all the latest news and releases (plus pictures of the aforementioned rescue pets)! Sign up for her newsletter at: http://eepurl.com/hkDlEP and follow her on social media!

WHAT'S NEXT?

Coming in 2022 from Falstaff Books, the re-launch of my werewolf secret agent urban fantasy series, The Rick Keller Project.

Cold Run

When you're a supernatural nuke, there's no such thing as retirement.

Rick Keller—prodigal son, loyal soldier, secret agent, and now cranky werewolf—just wants to be left alone. When MONIKER, the shadowy organization he once worked for, returns him forcefully to active service, he has a choice: follow orders or spend the rest of his life chained to a lab table in the basement.

Thrown onto a team with two strangers—an angry ex-cop and an agent with a past almost as shady as his—Rick is back on the hunt, running down human traffickers for his government minders. But he's been out of the game a long time. His instincts are rusty.

And there's no escaping the shadows of his past, no matter how fast he runs.